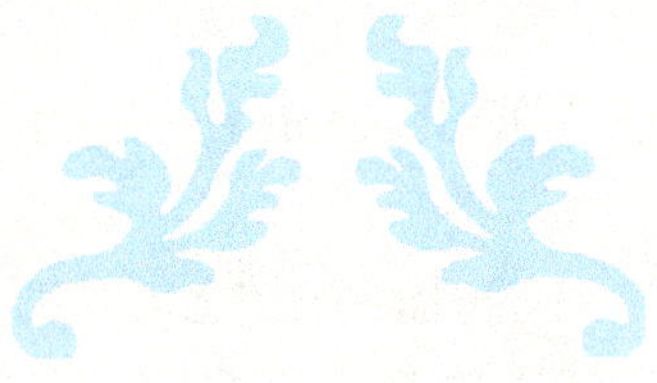

NAUGHTY NUDIES OF 1908:

A GLIMPSE OF VICTORIAN EROTICA

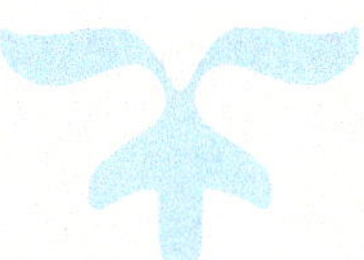

By
Uma Bouschertz

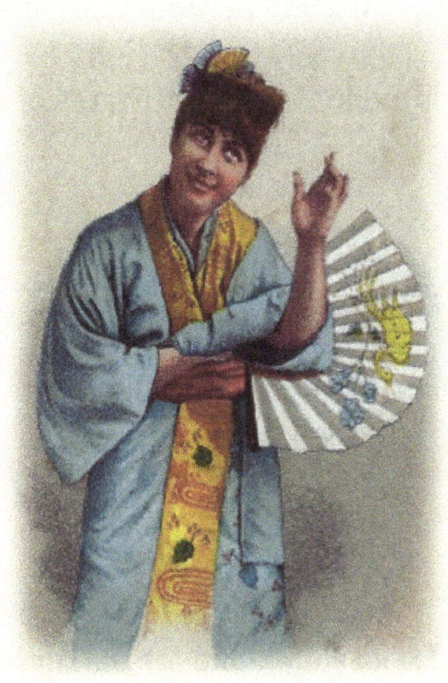

DECEMBER 1, 2013

DARKER INTENTIONS PRESS
POB 569, Freehold, NJ 07728

Naughty Nudies of 1908: A Glimpse of Victorian Erotica

Published by
DARKER INTENTIONS PRESS
POB 569
FREEHOLD,NJ 07728

Any resemblance of to any persons living is purely coincidental as all these people are as dead as doornails and have been so for at least a hundred years... This book is a complete work of fiction.

Proudly Printed in the United States of American

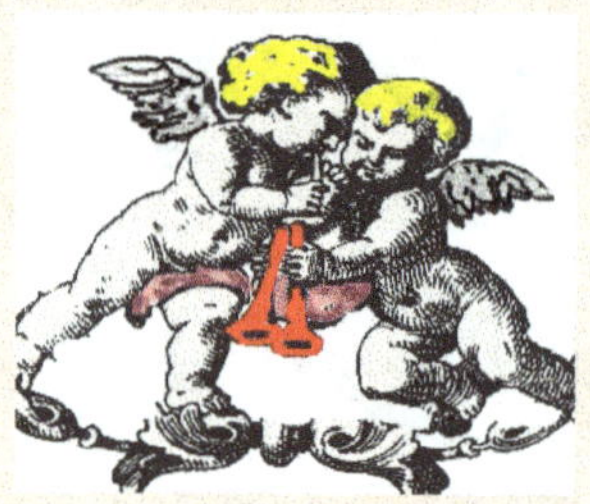

Layout and Design Exclusively done for Darker Intentions Press by
SOBEE STUDIO

ISBN: 978-0-9827597-4-5

BEAUTIFUL LADIES

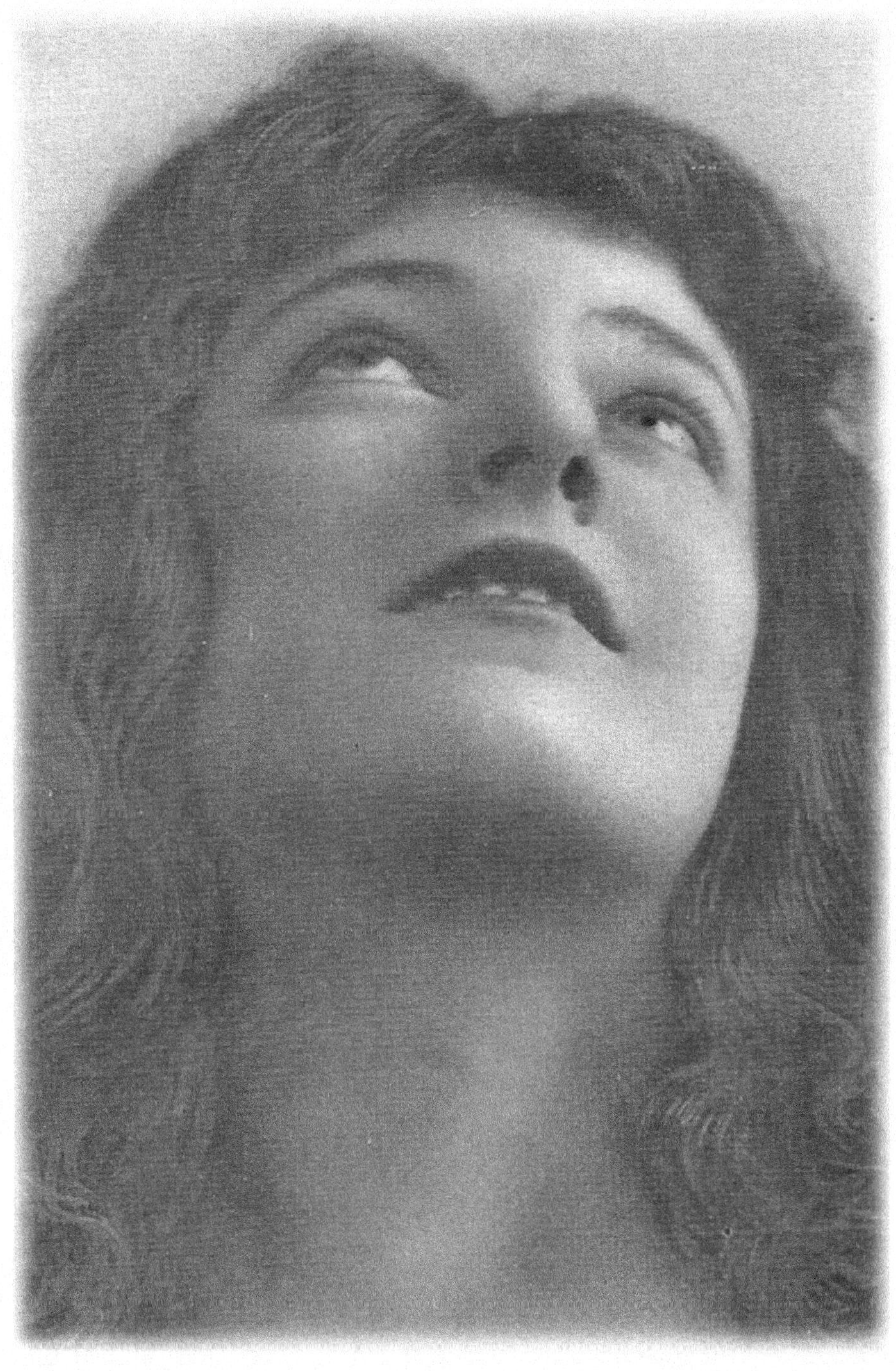

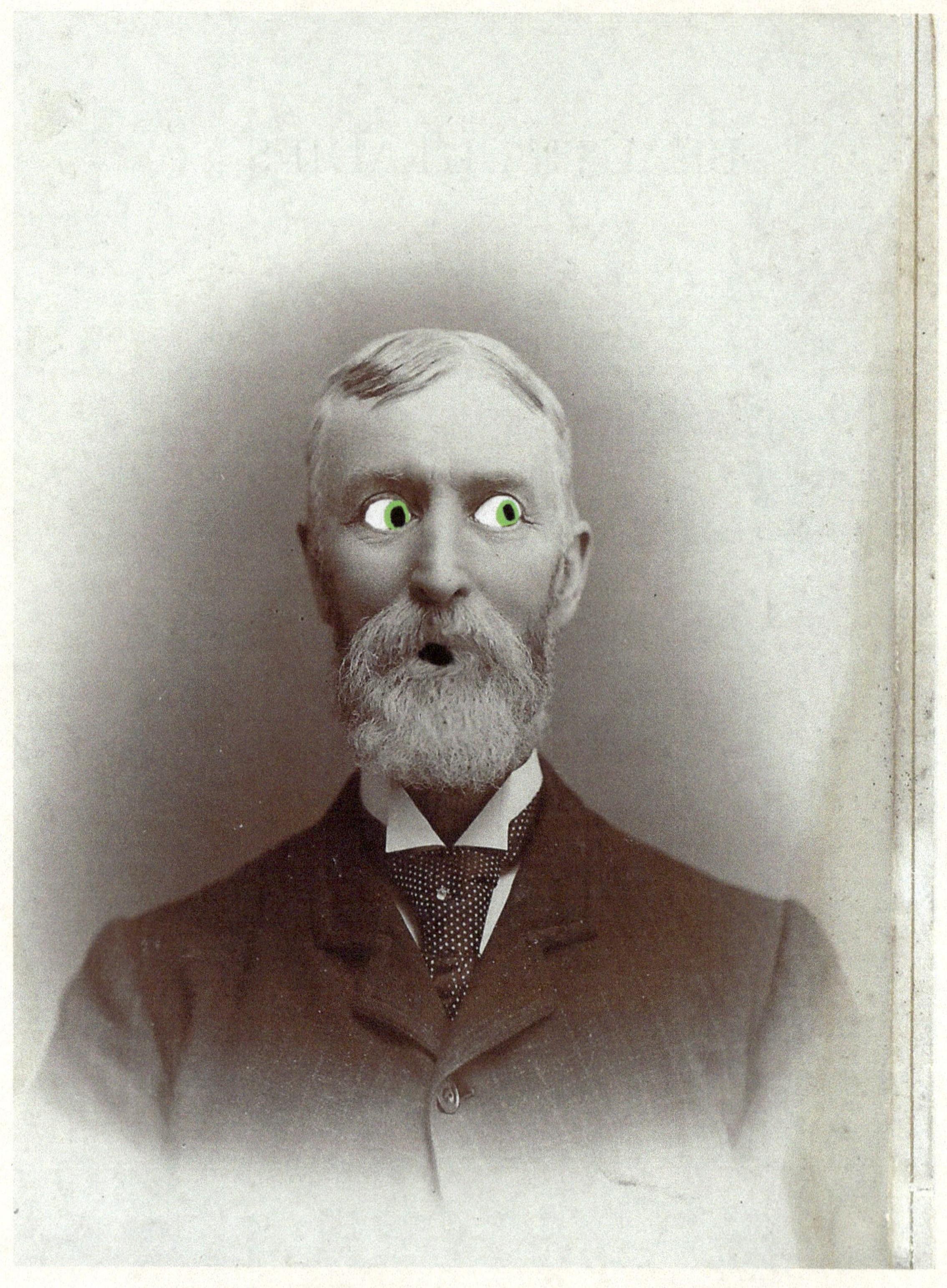

And so Mr. Chigpiddle did not approve of the girl's activities...

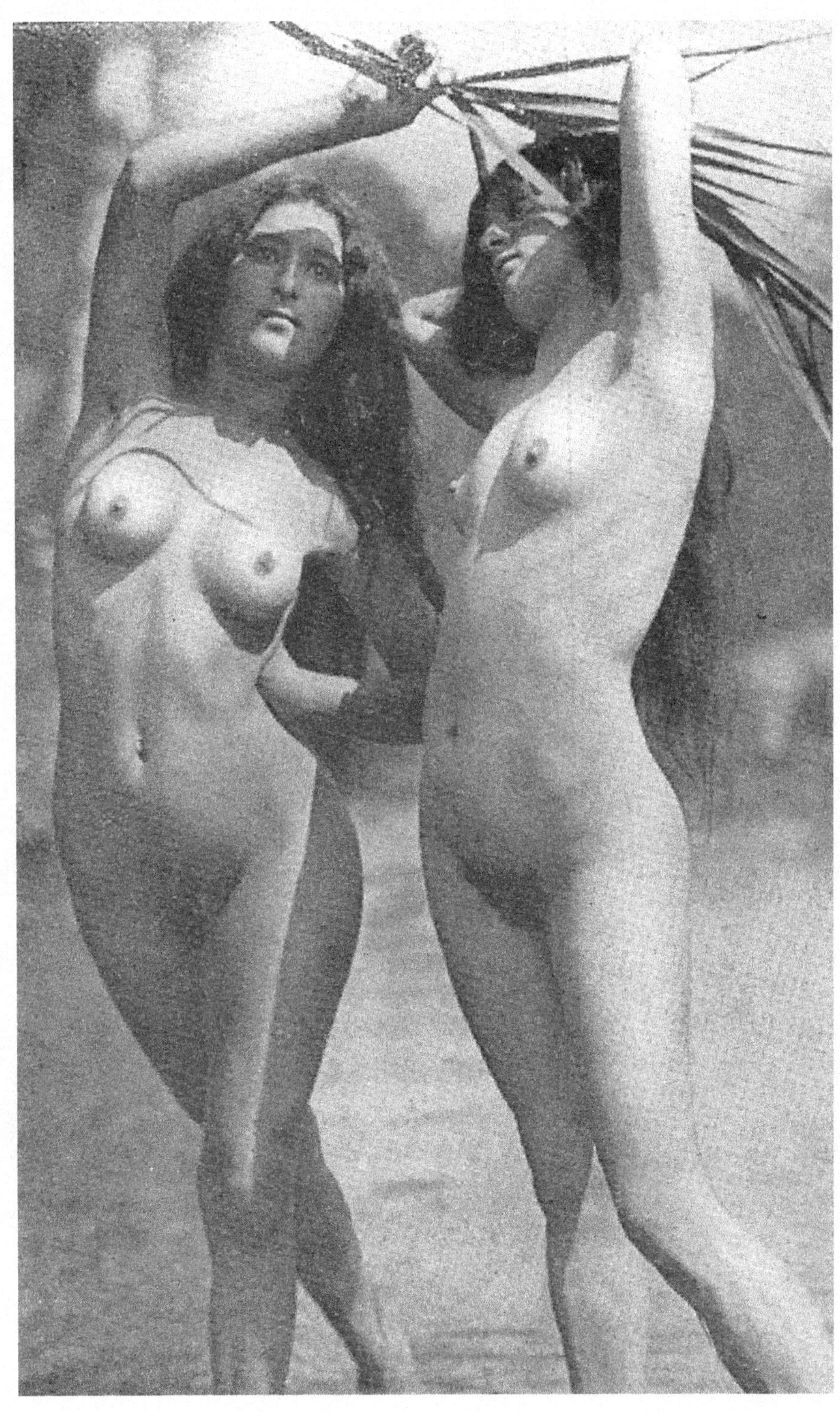

Watersports were not his thing…

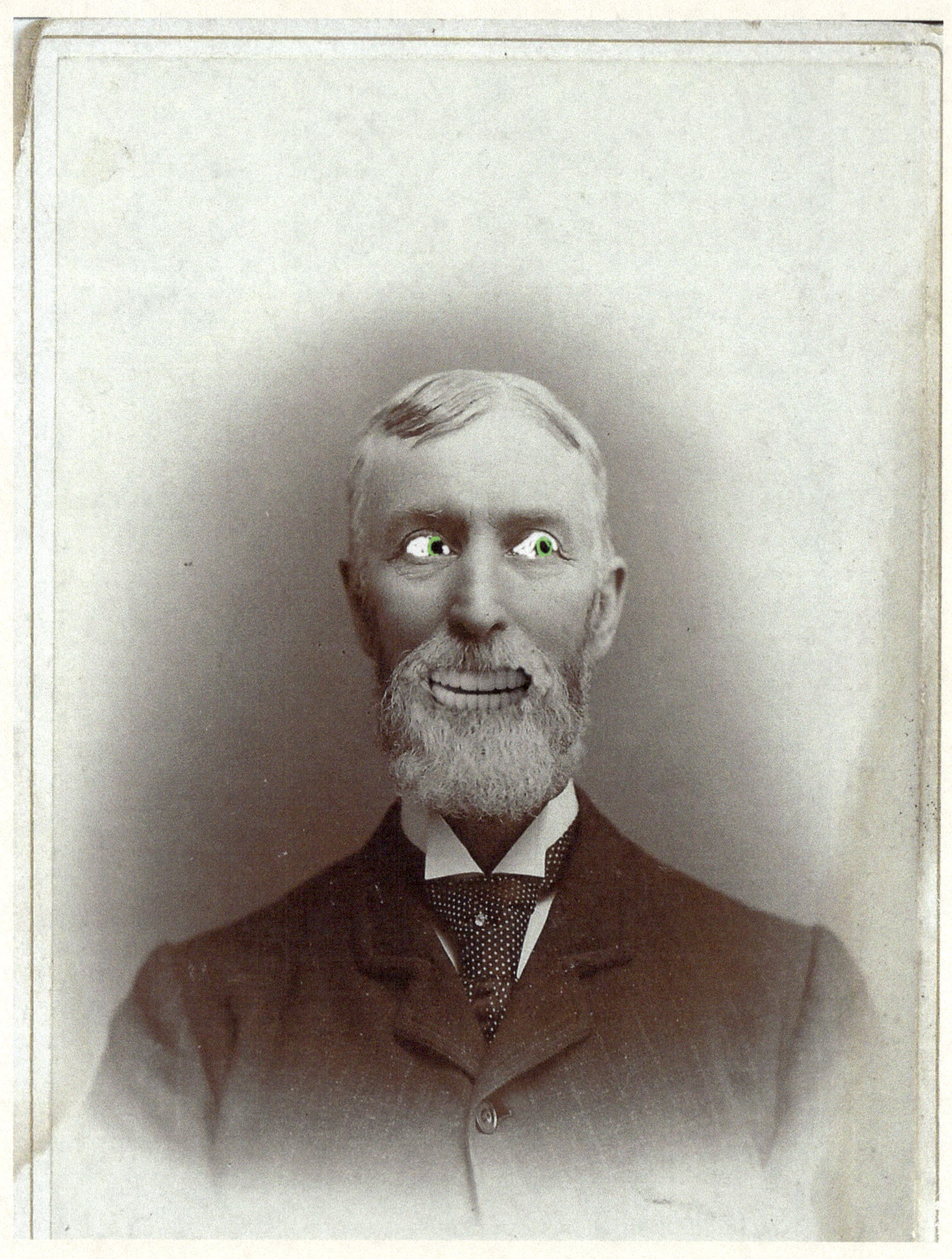

But Mr. Chigpiddle kept watching anyway…

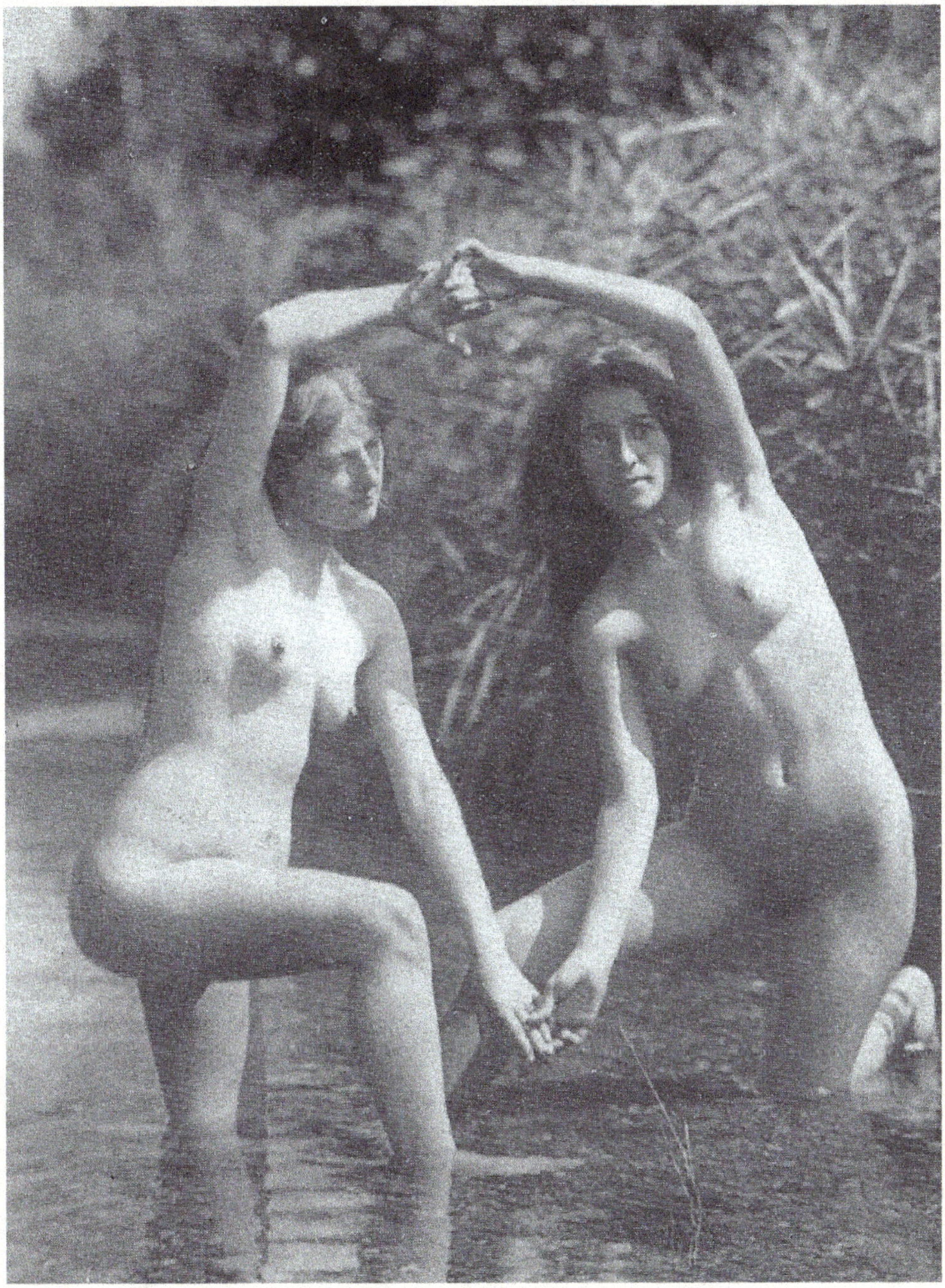

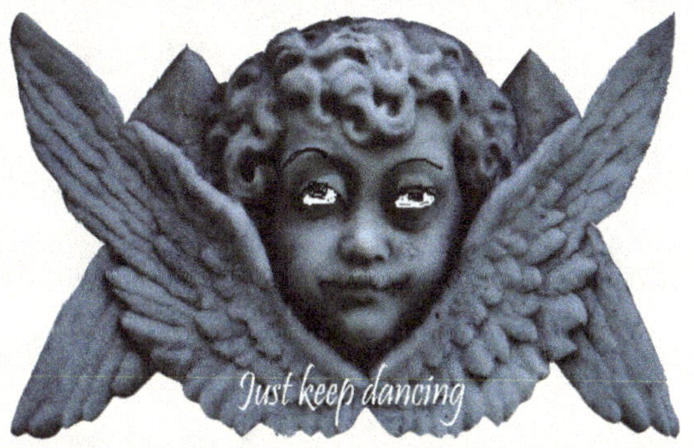
Just keep dancing

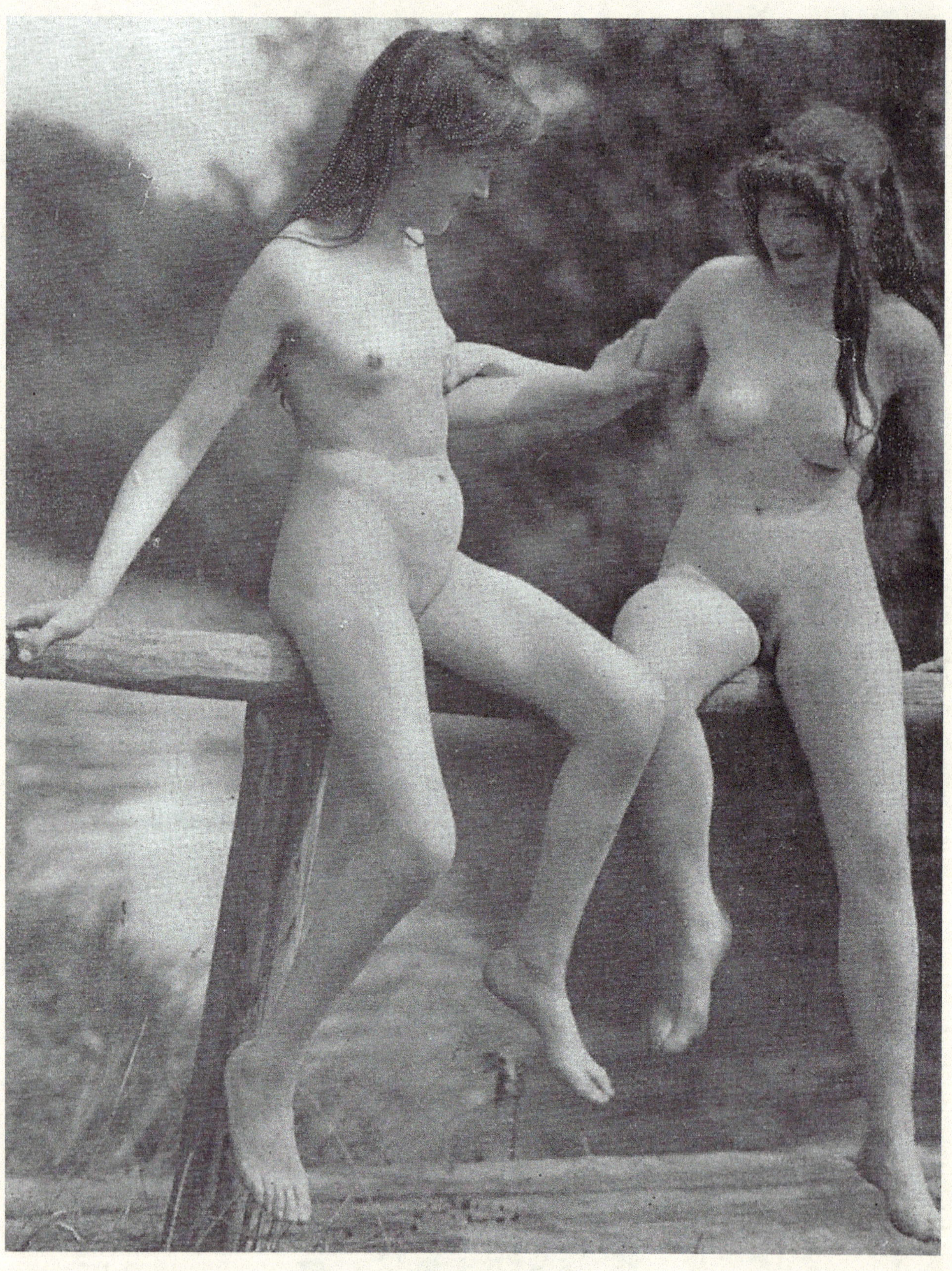

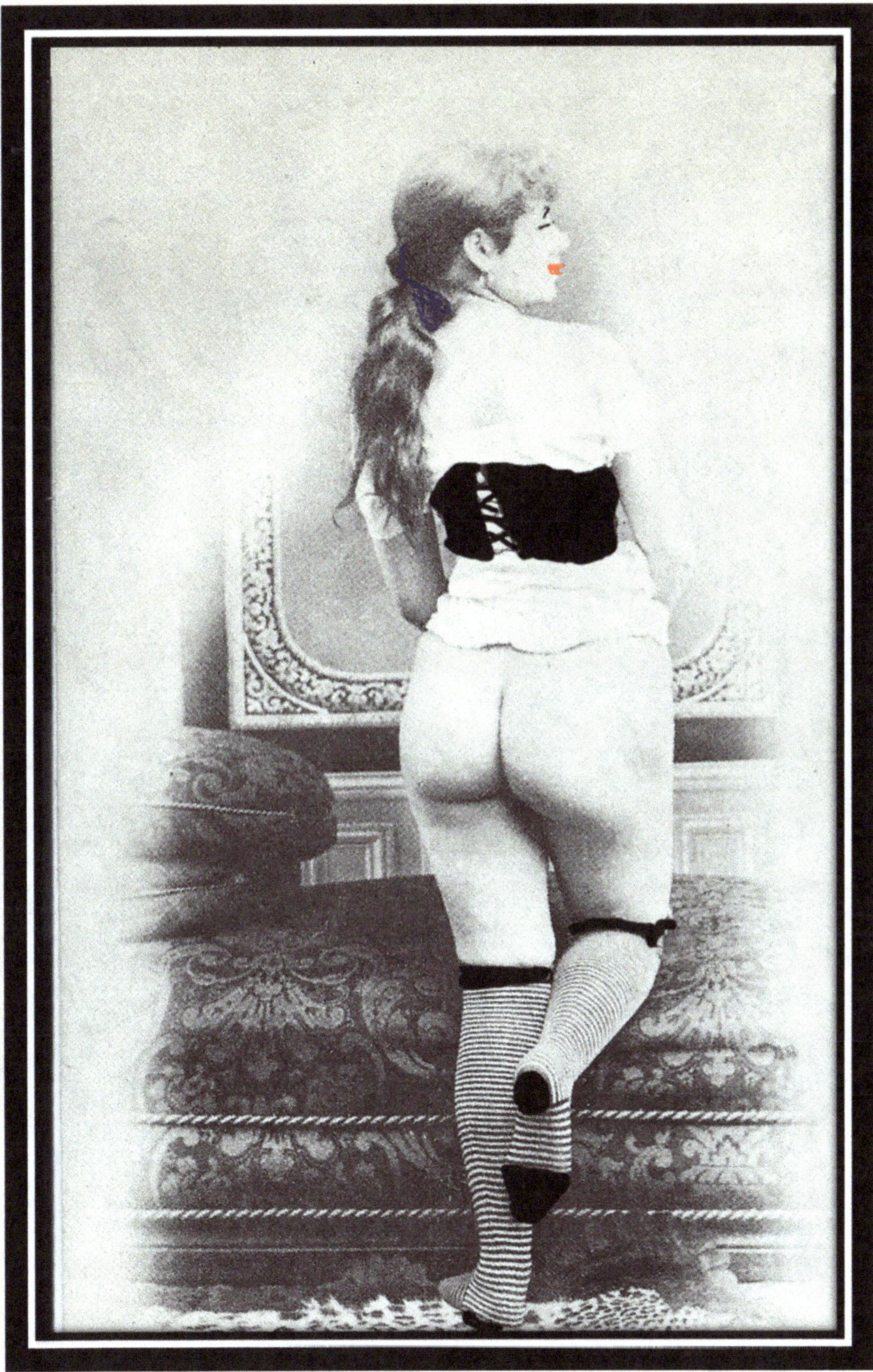

No Butts

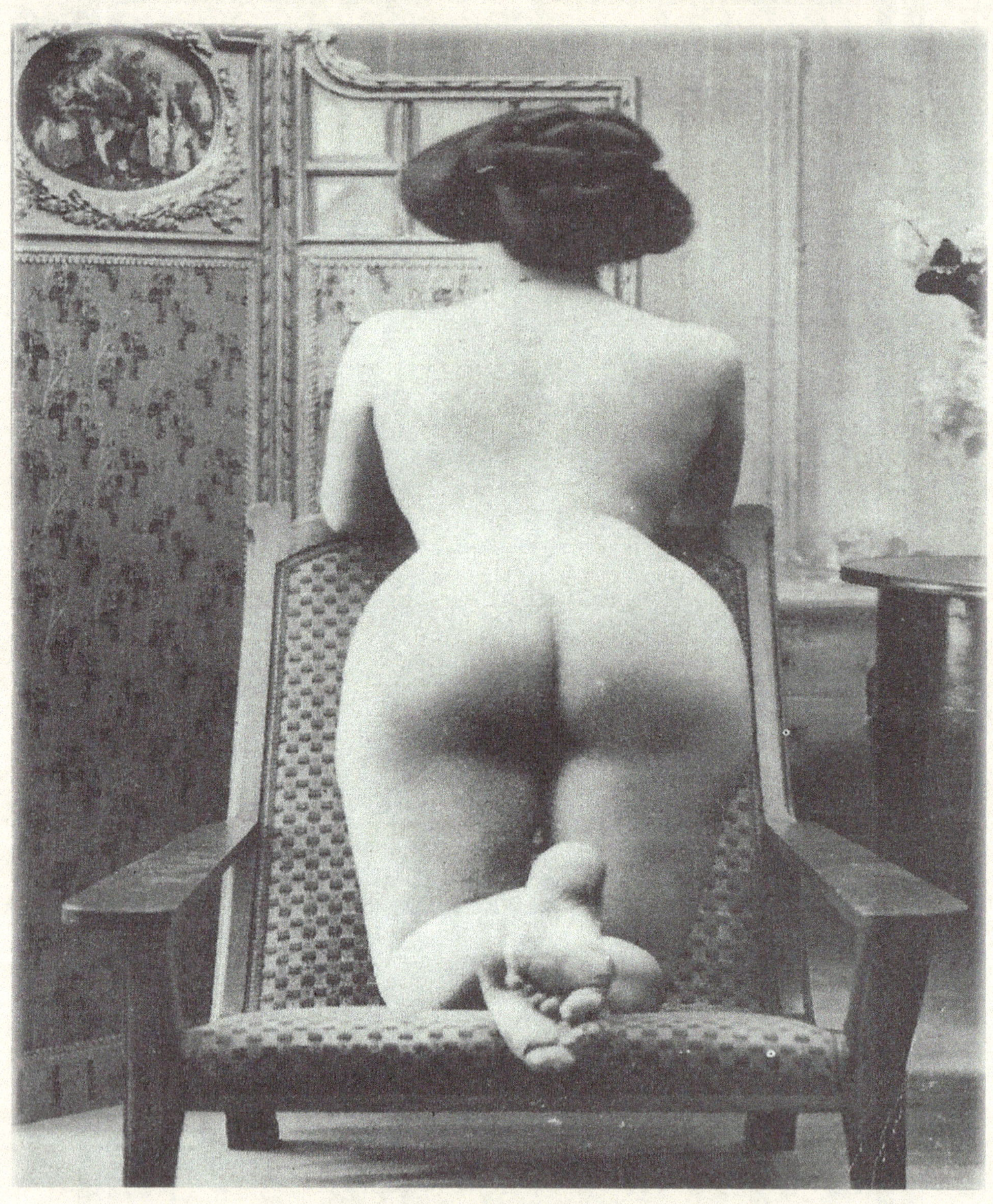

…About it!

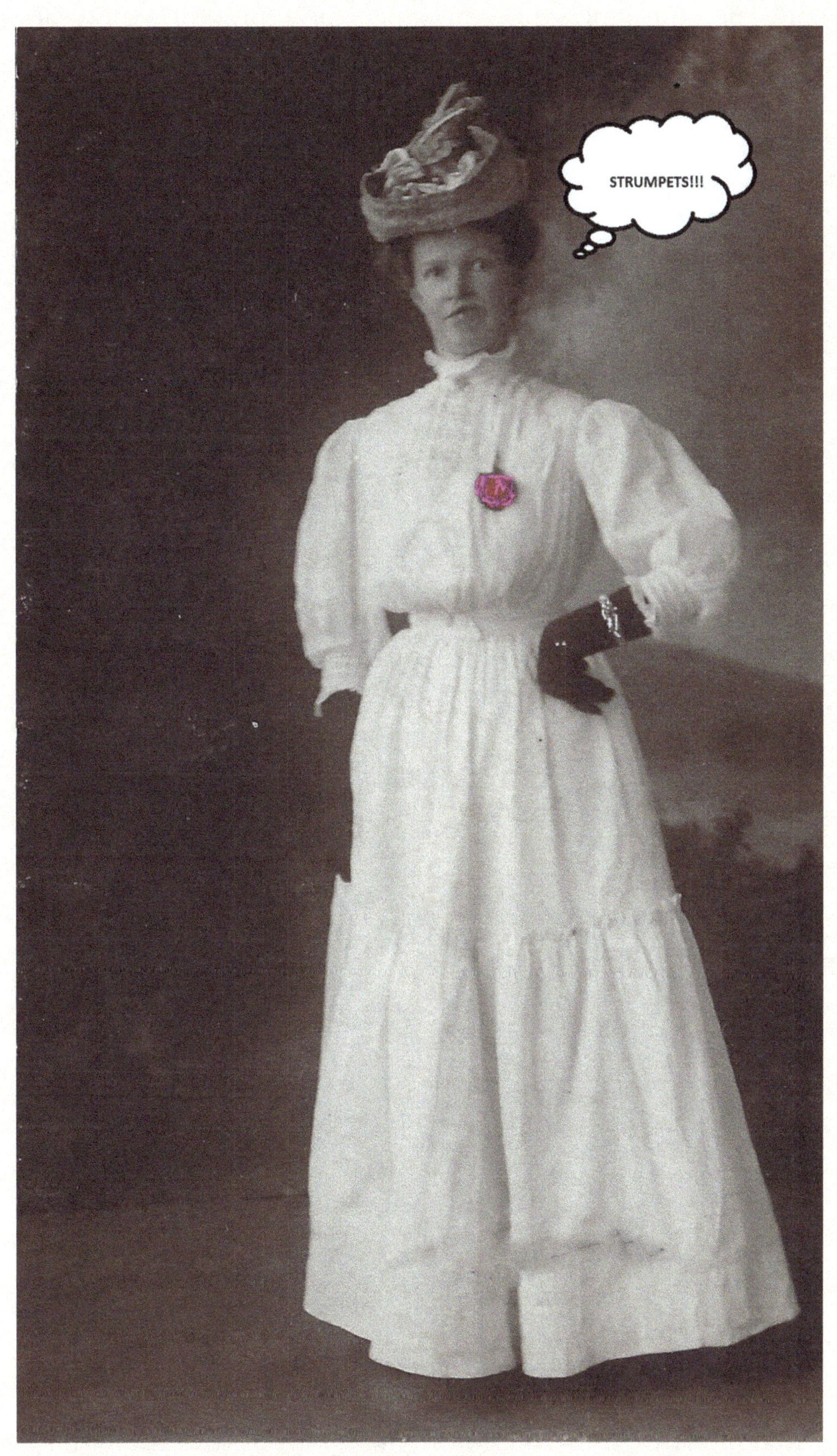
STRUMPETS!!!

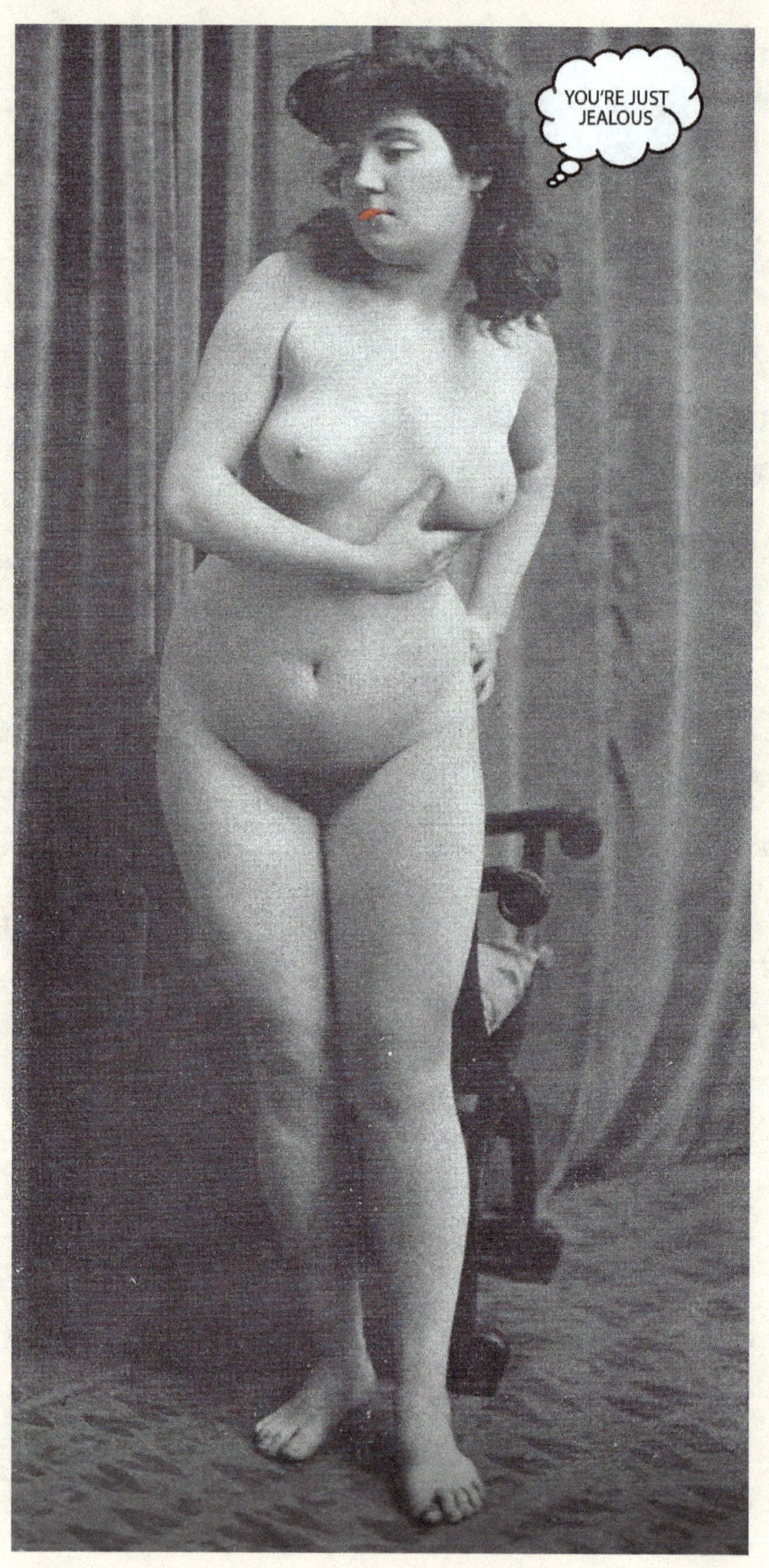
YOU'RE JUST JEALOUS

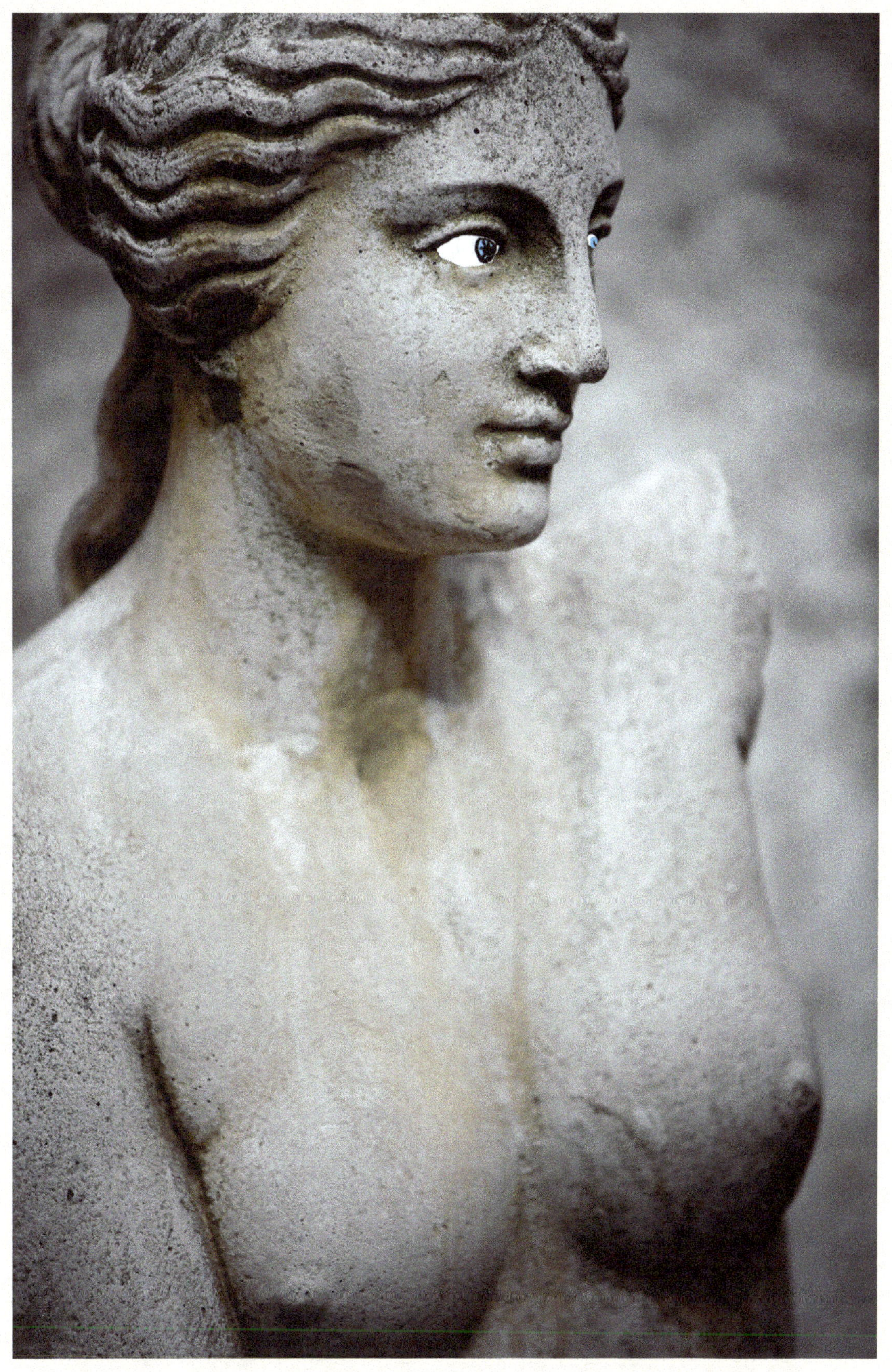

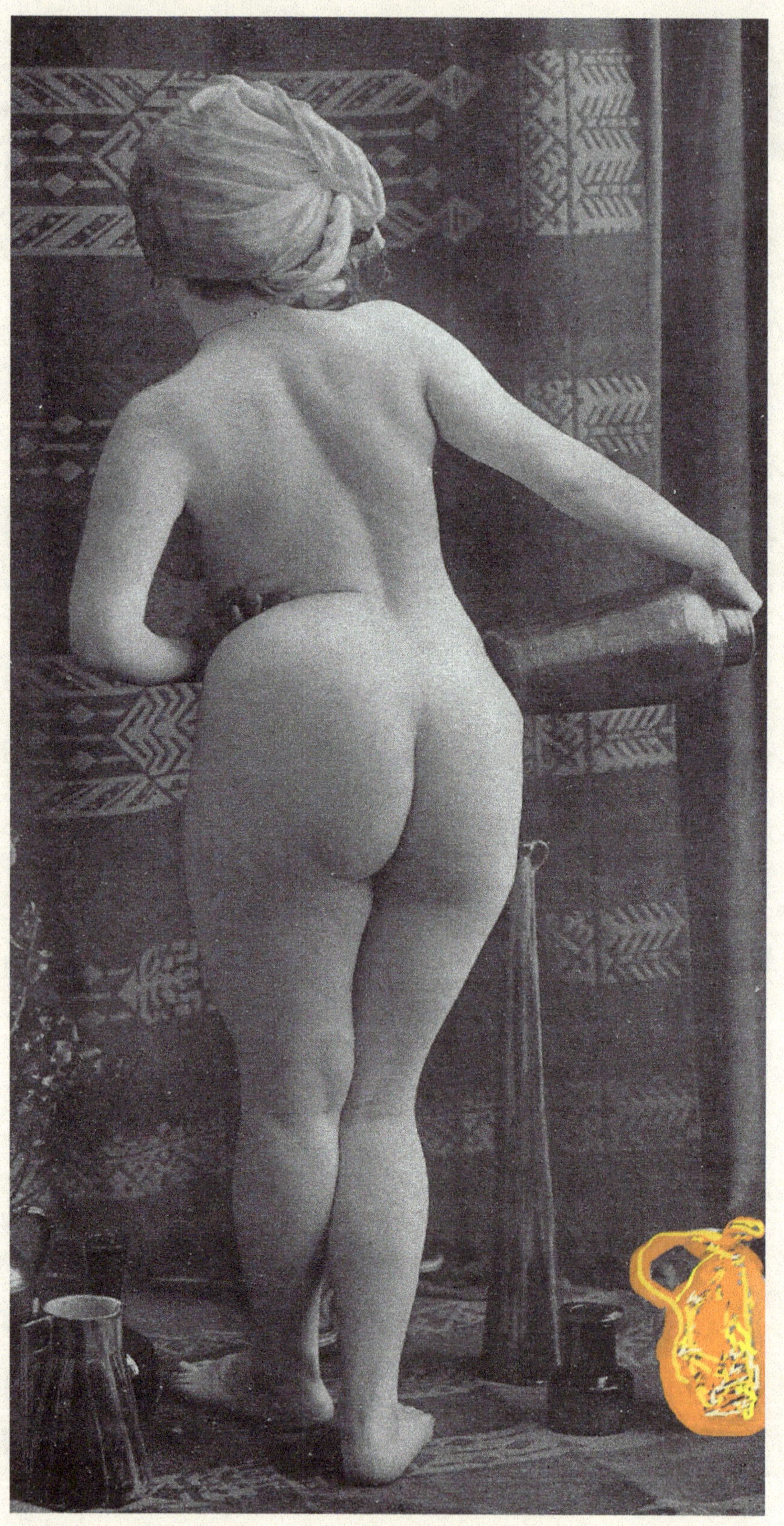

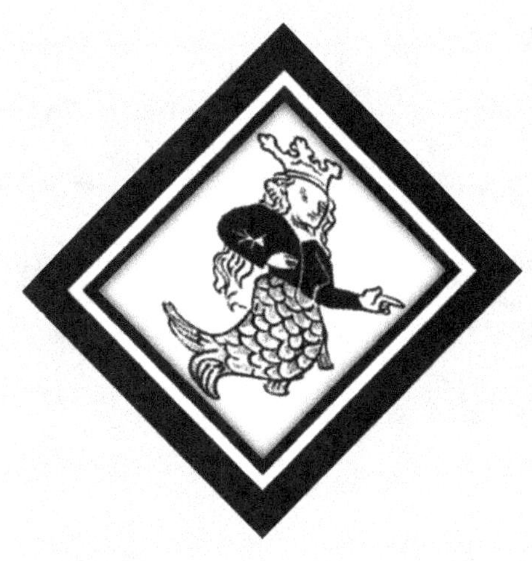

QUEENS OF THE WOOD

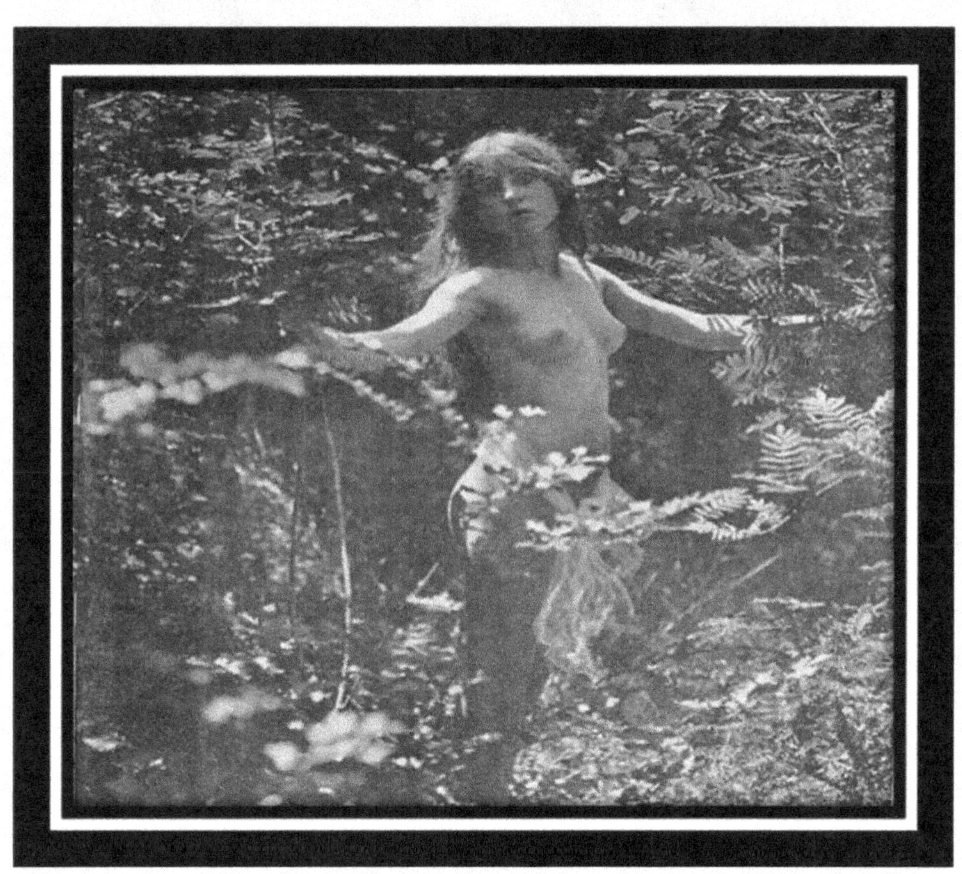

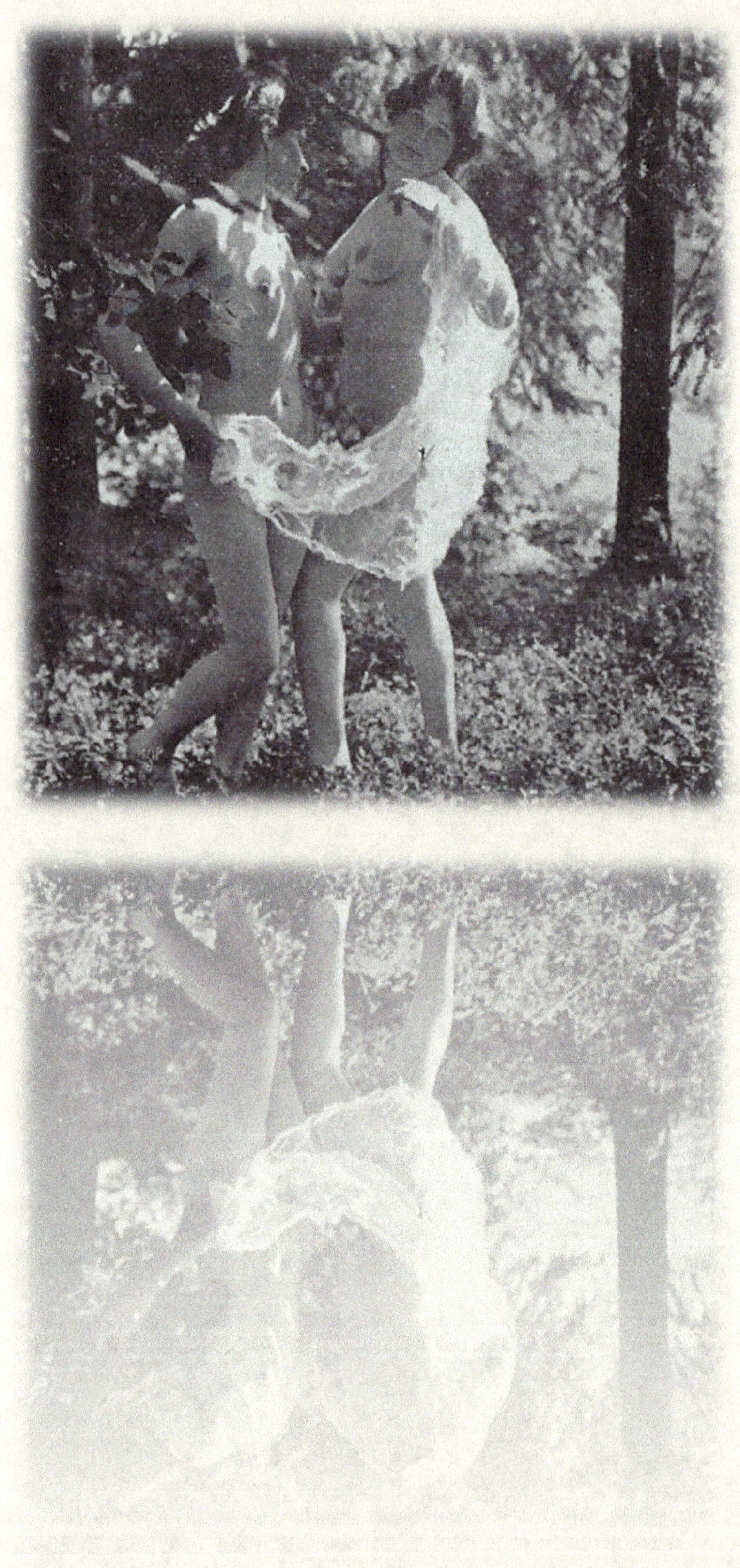

reflections

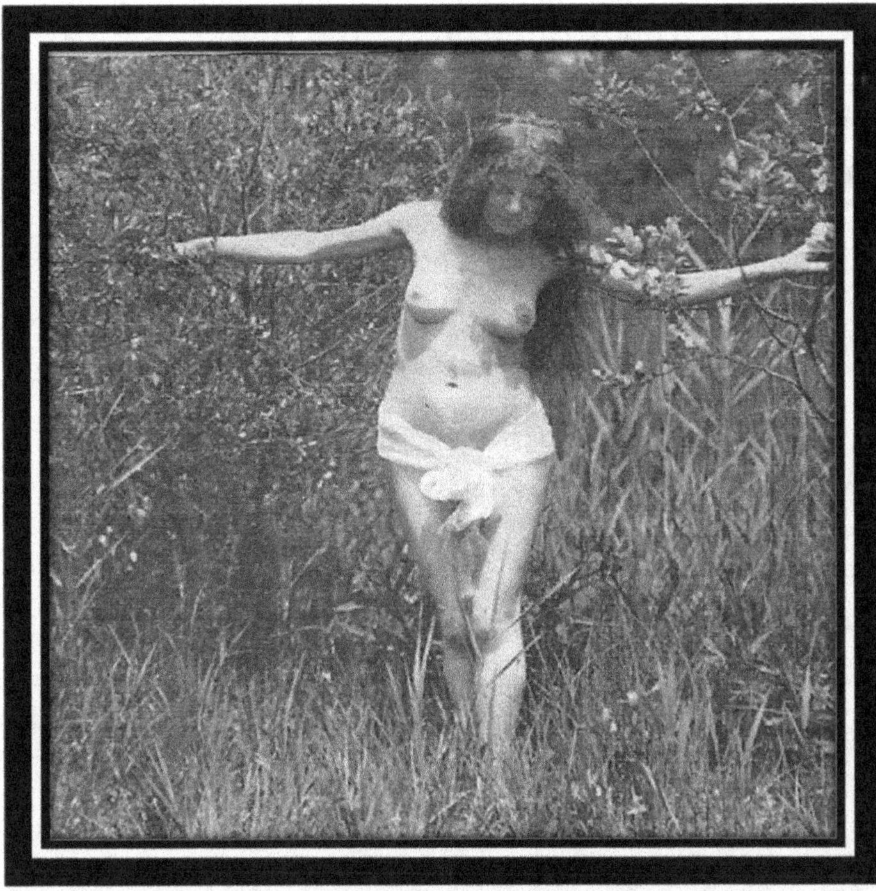

Chester and Venus were always the Life of the Party...

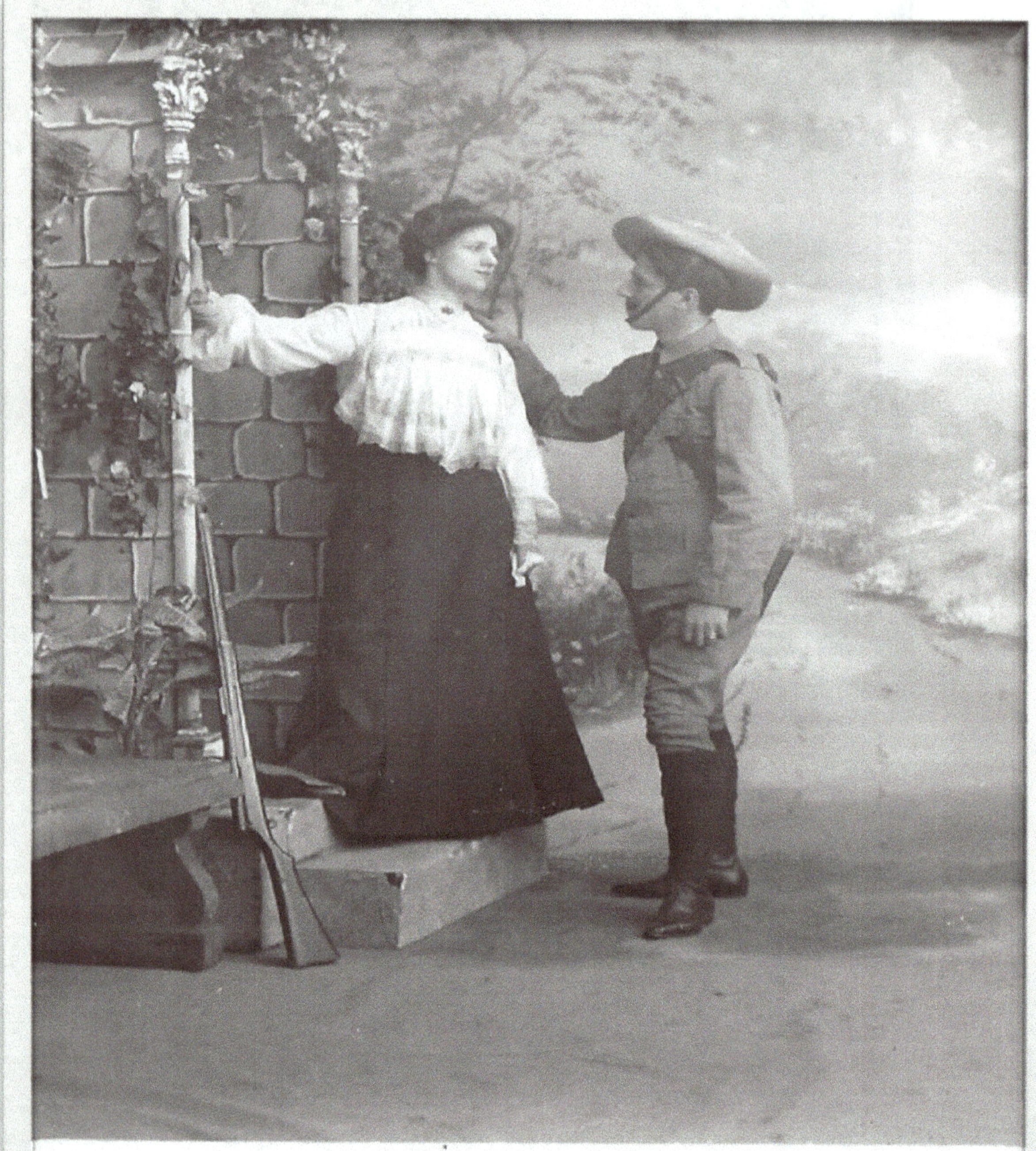

9253 'NEATH THE HAWTHORNS 3. ROTARY PHOTO, E.C.

Glorious spring at last has come again, and all is bright and gay,
As down the sunny village street ride the heroes of the fray.
All weary waiting is over now, 'neath the hawthorns they have met,
And the love of old times burns anew, as he whispers to his pet

and so were Edith, Hester and Lolly!

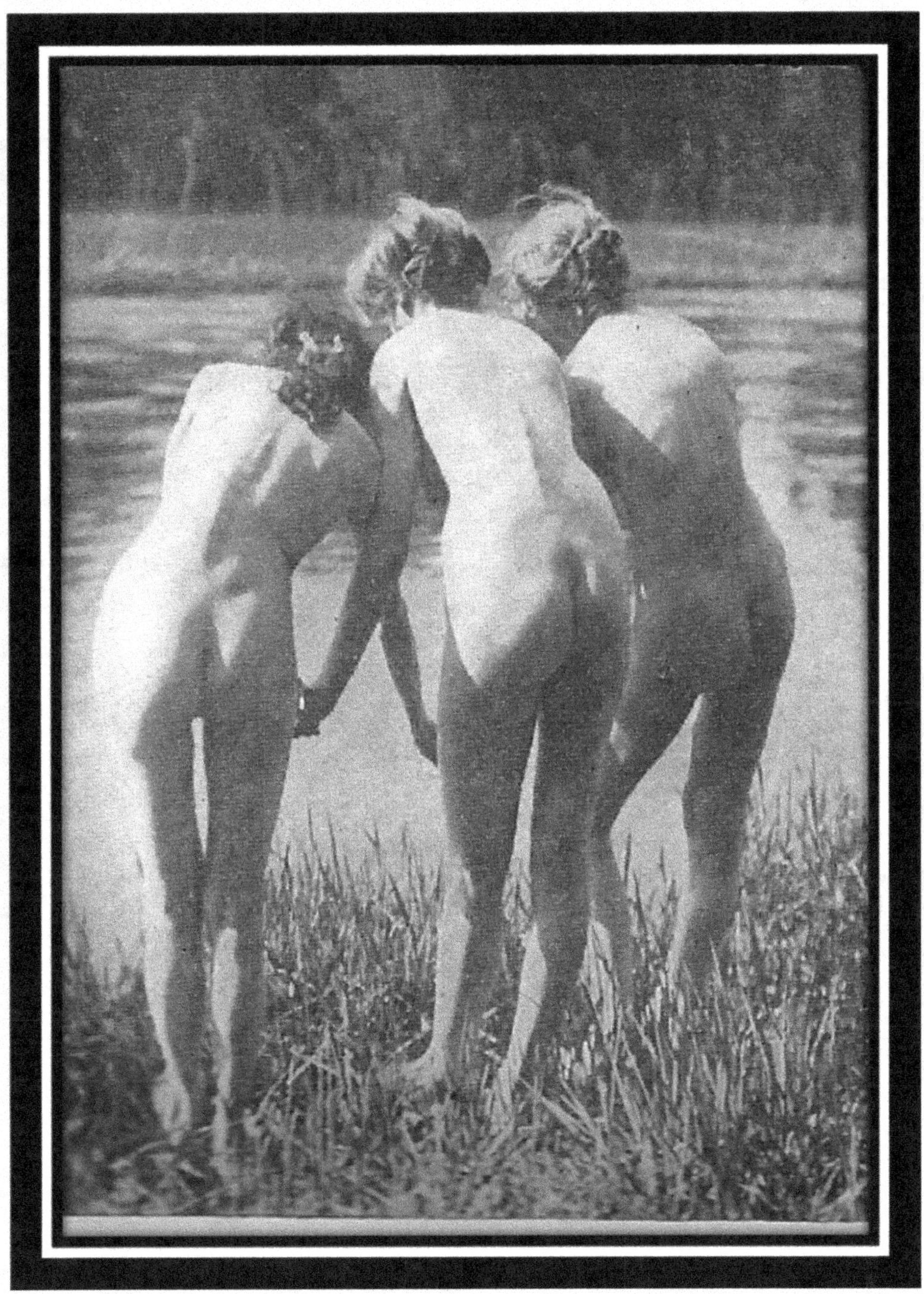

Three ladies down by the river...

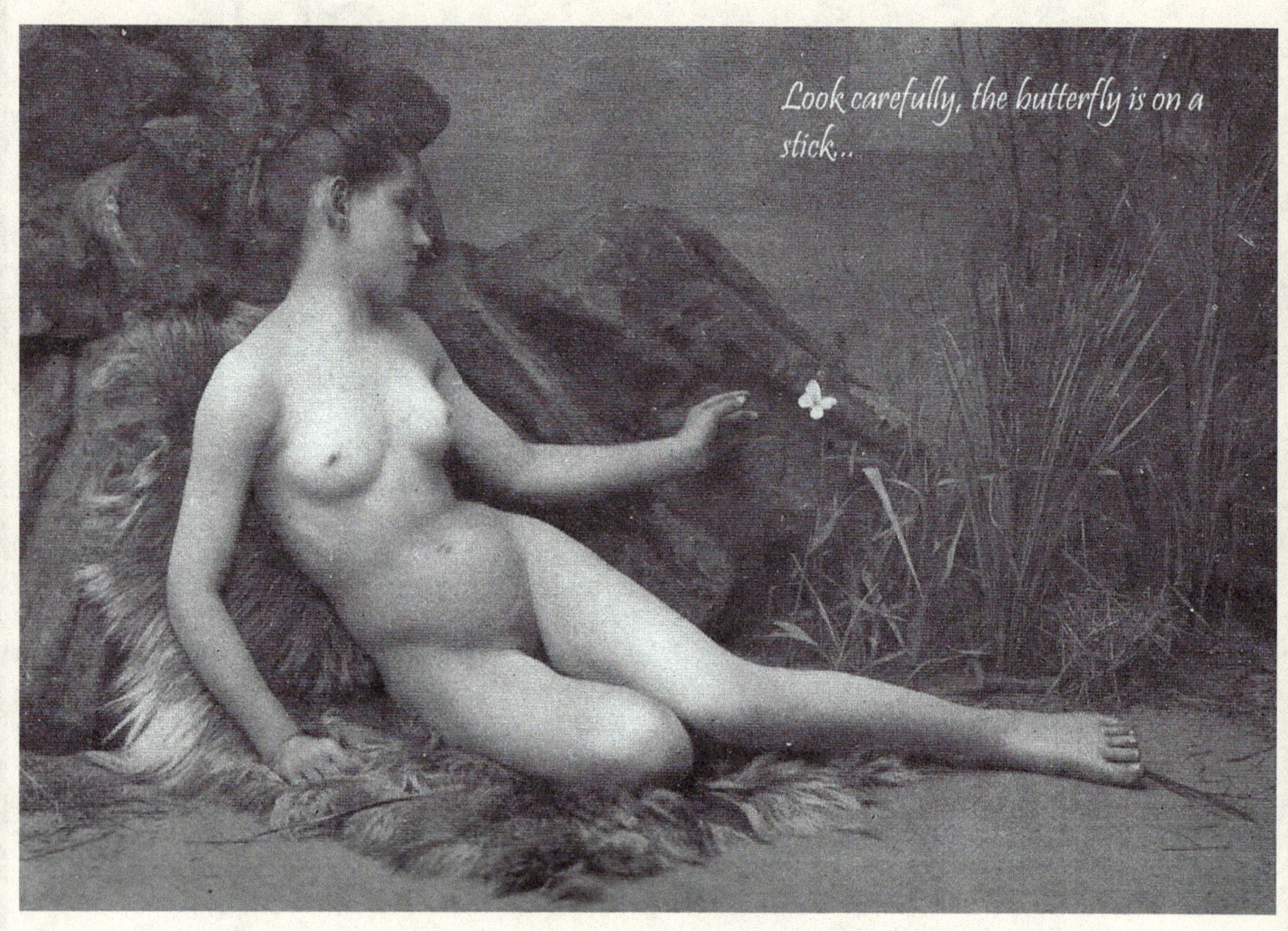
Look carefully, the butterfly is on a stick...

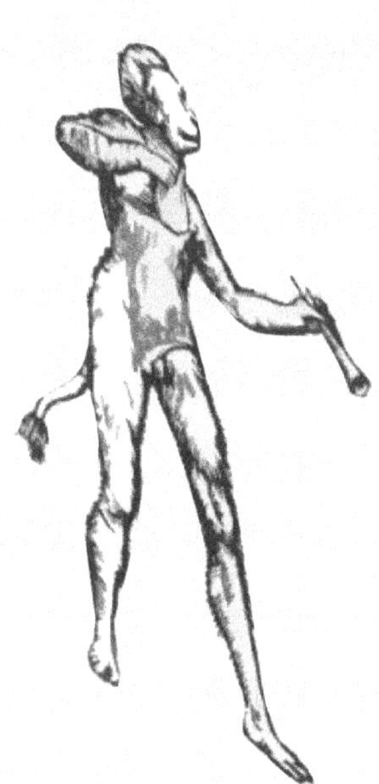

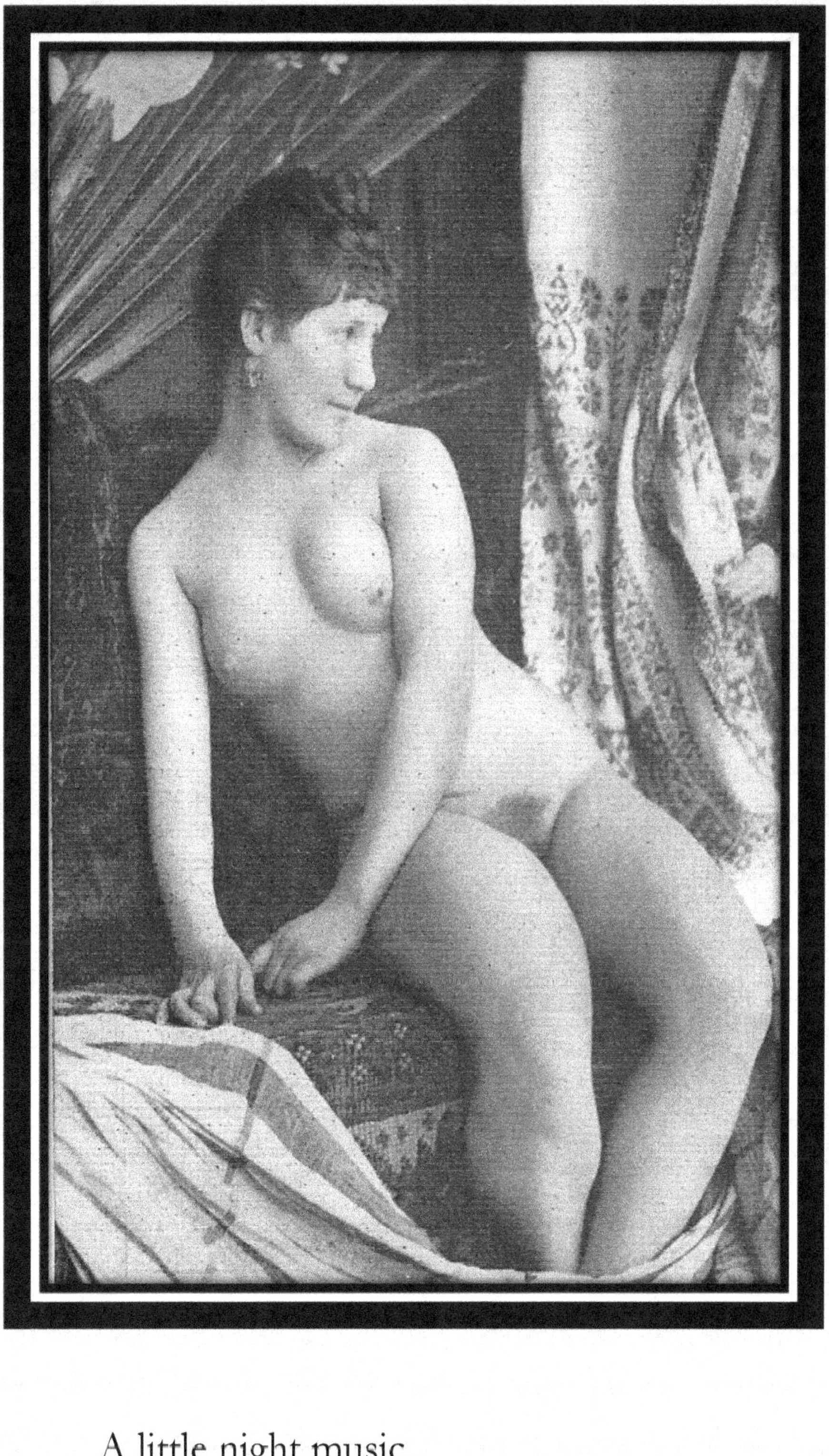

A little night music..

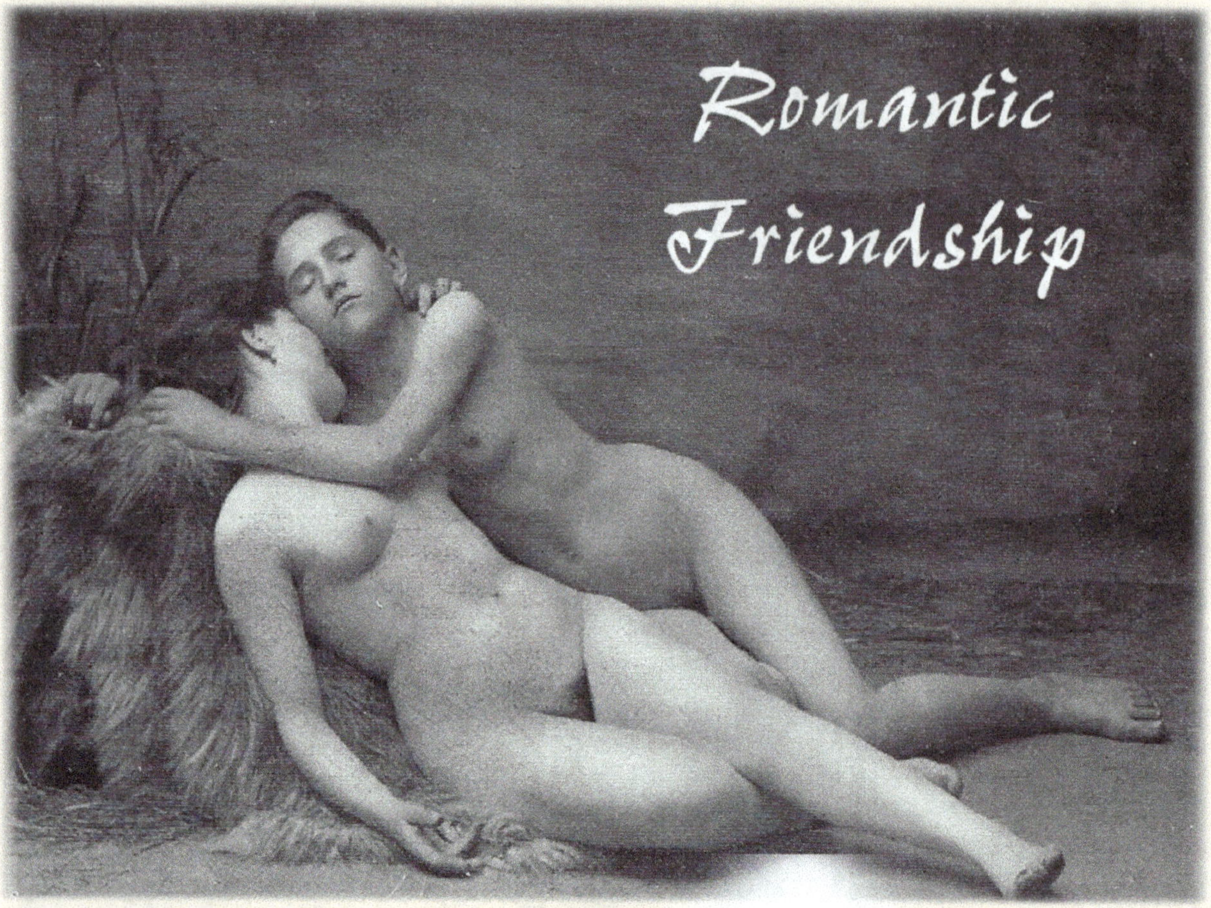

Romantic Friendship

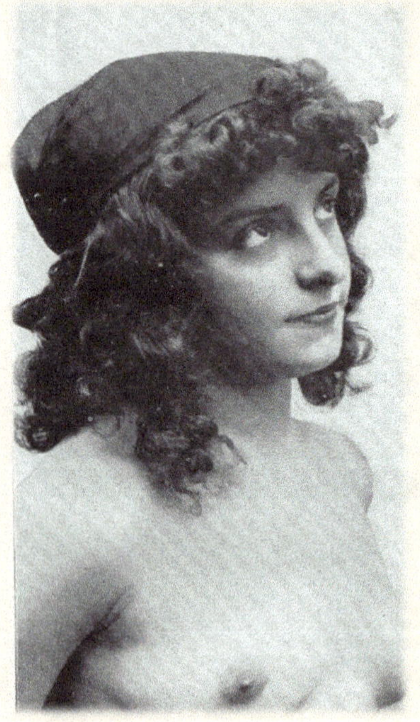

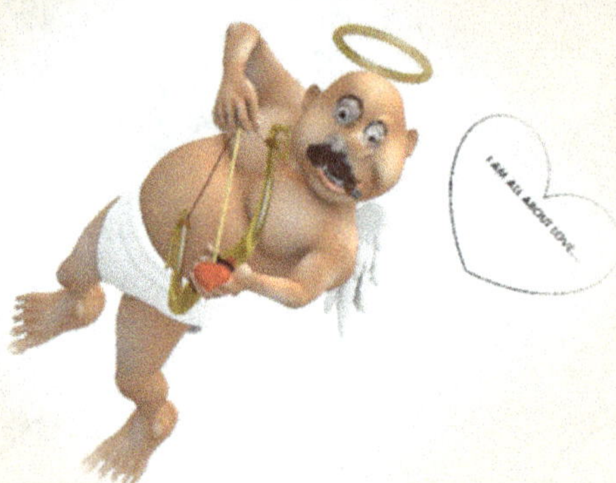

He's all about the love??

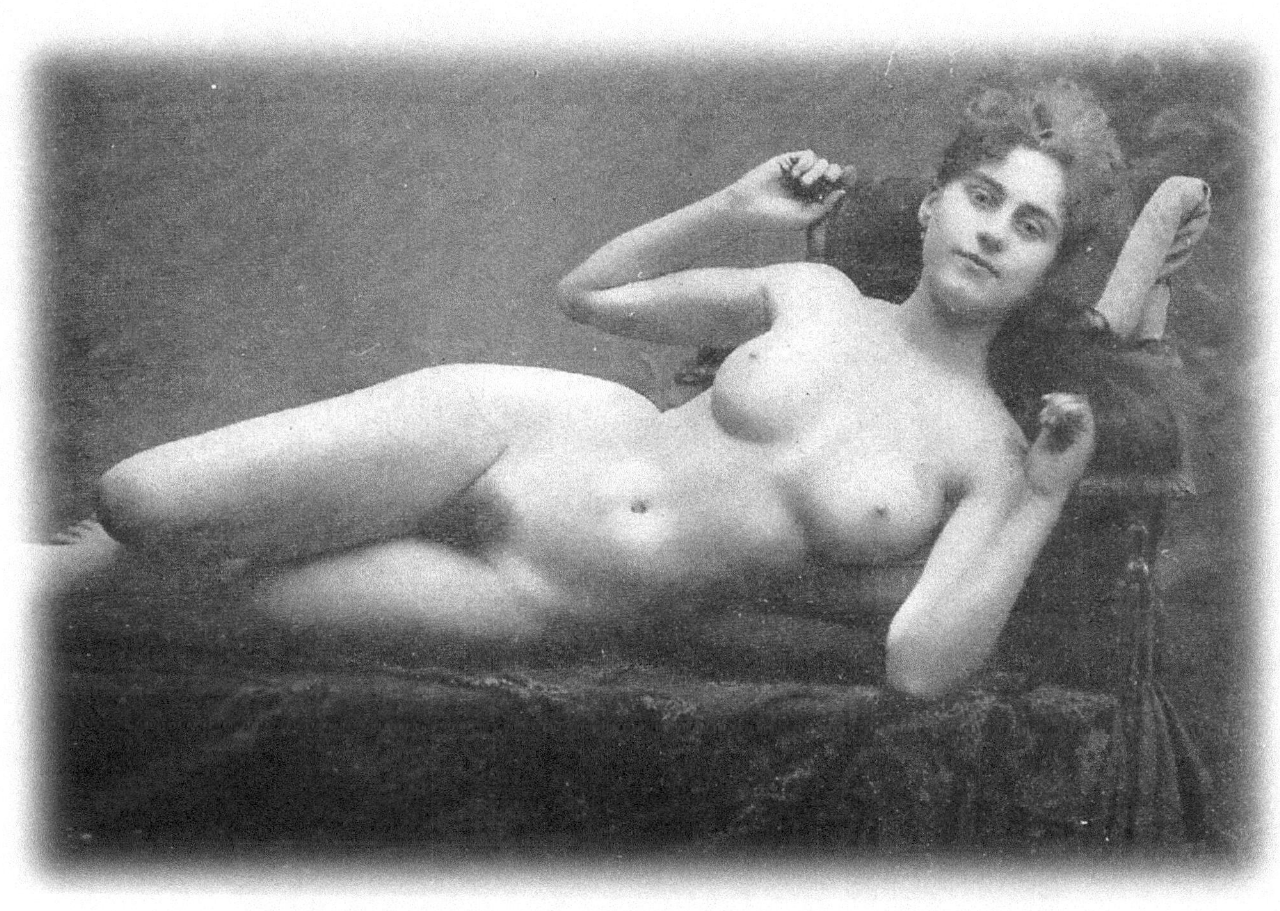

Alfreda remembered that day at the beach...

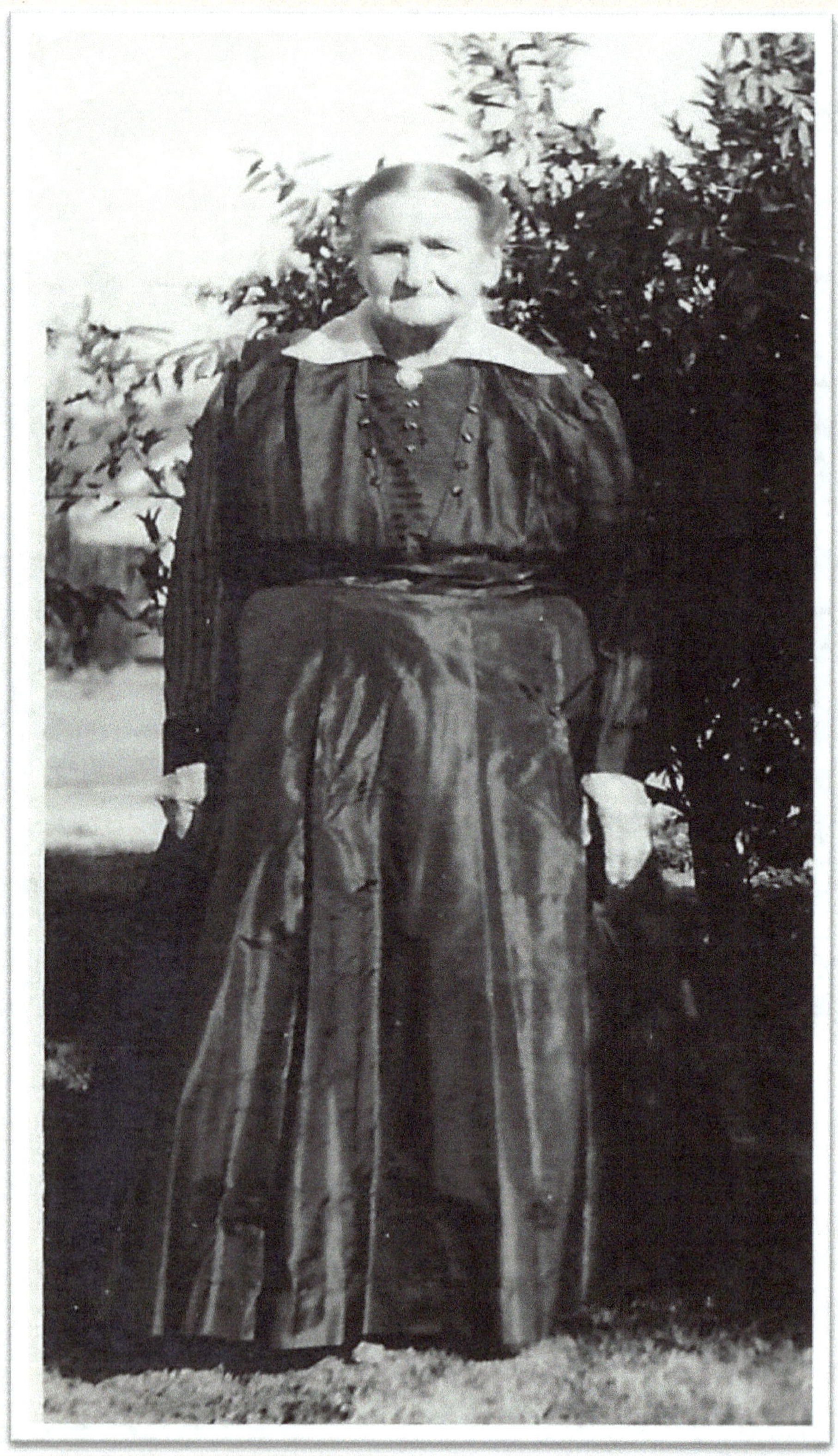

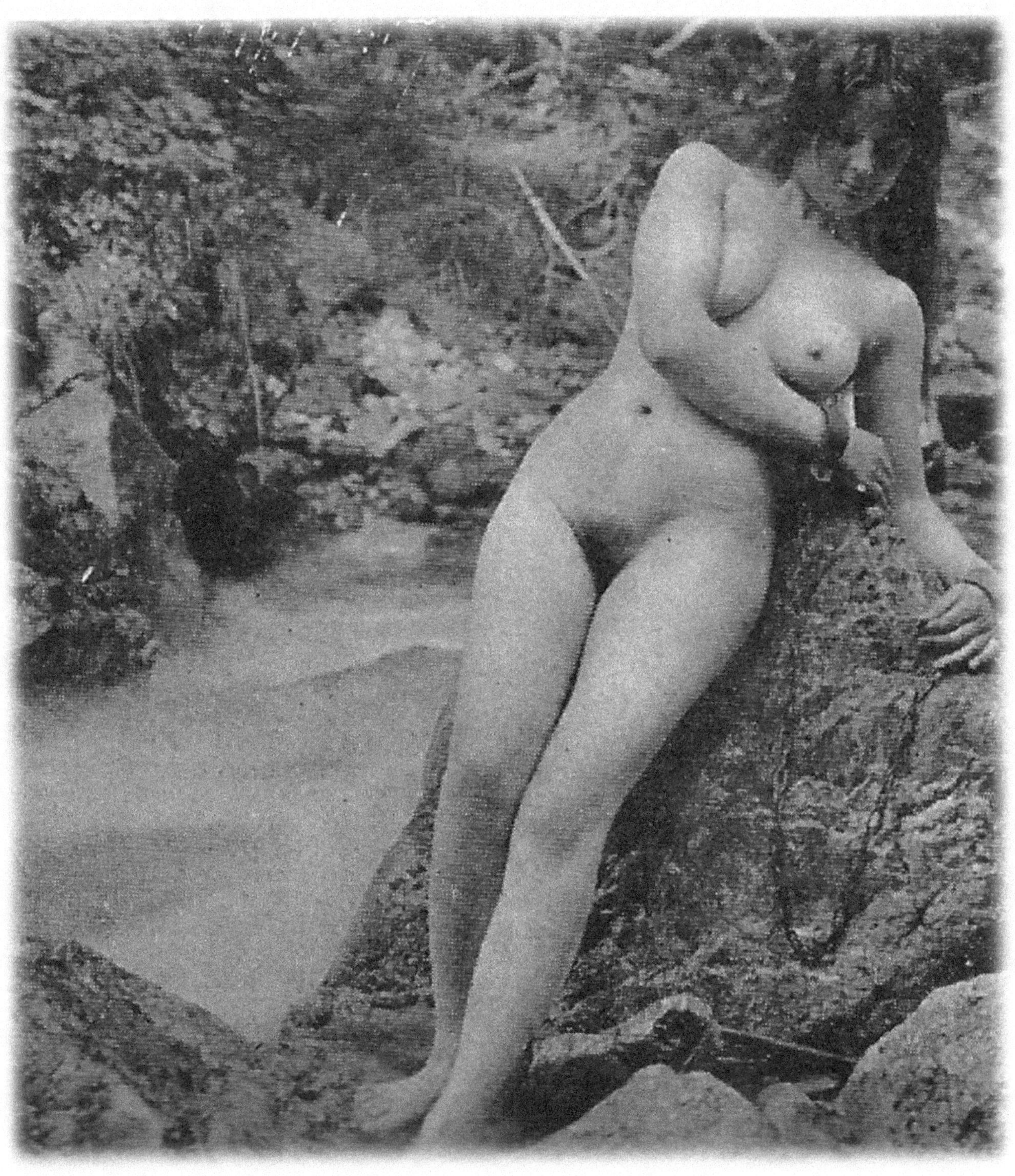

And down by the waterfall…with the chains

Wild sea-spray driven of the storm
Is not so wildly white as she,
Who beckoned with a foam-white arm
To me..

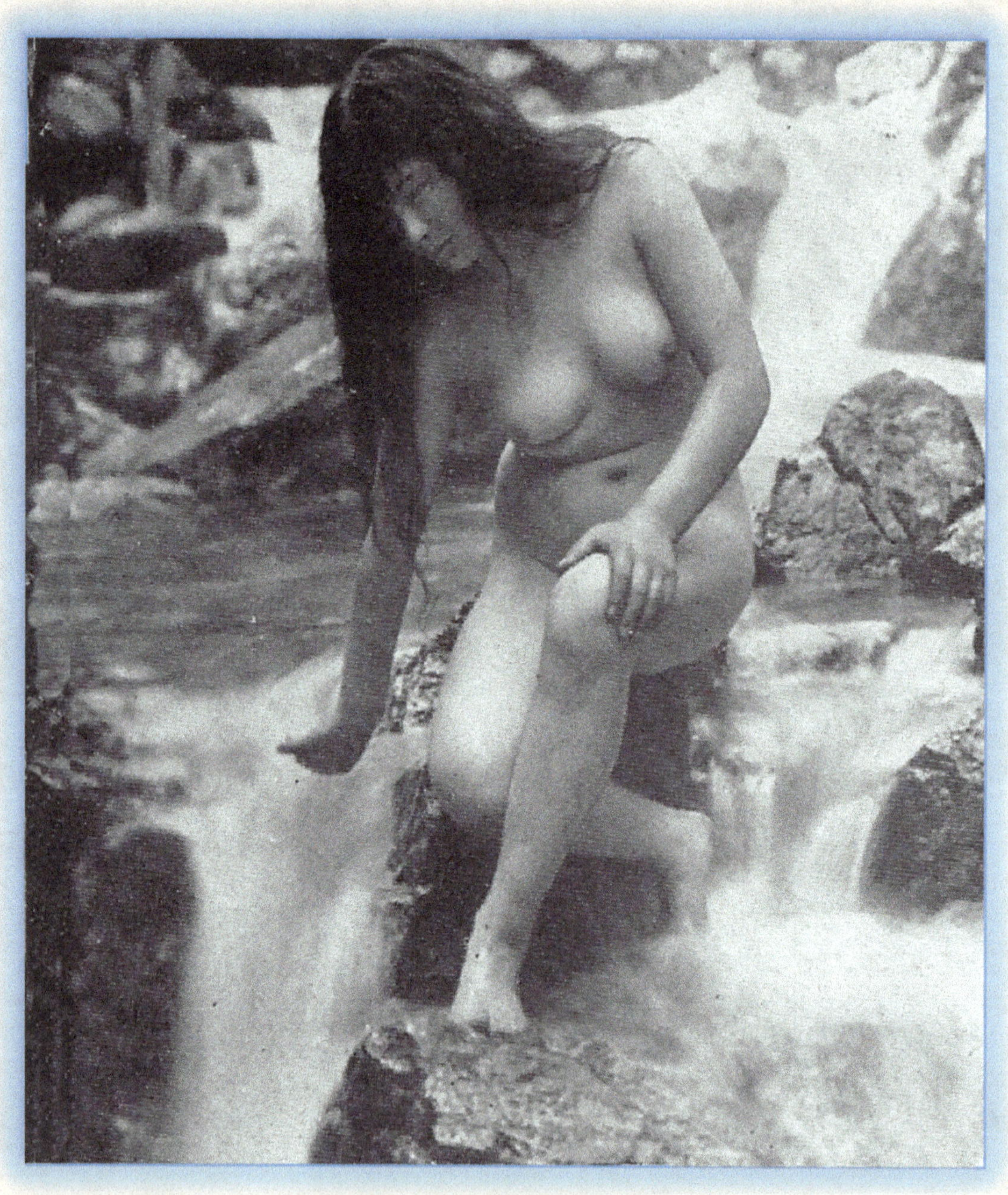

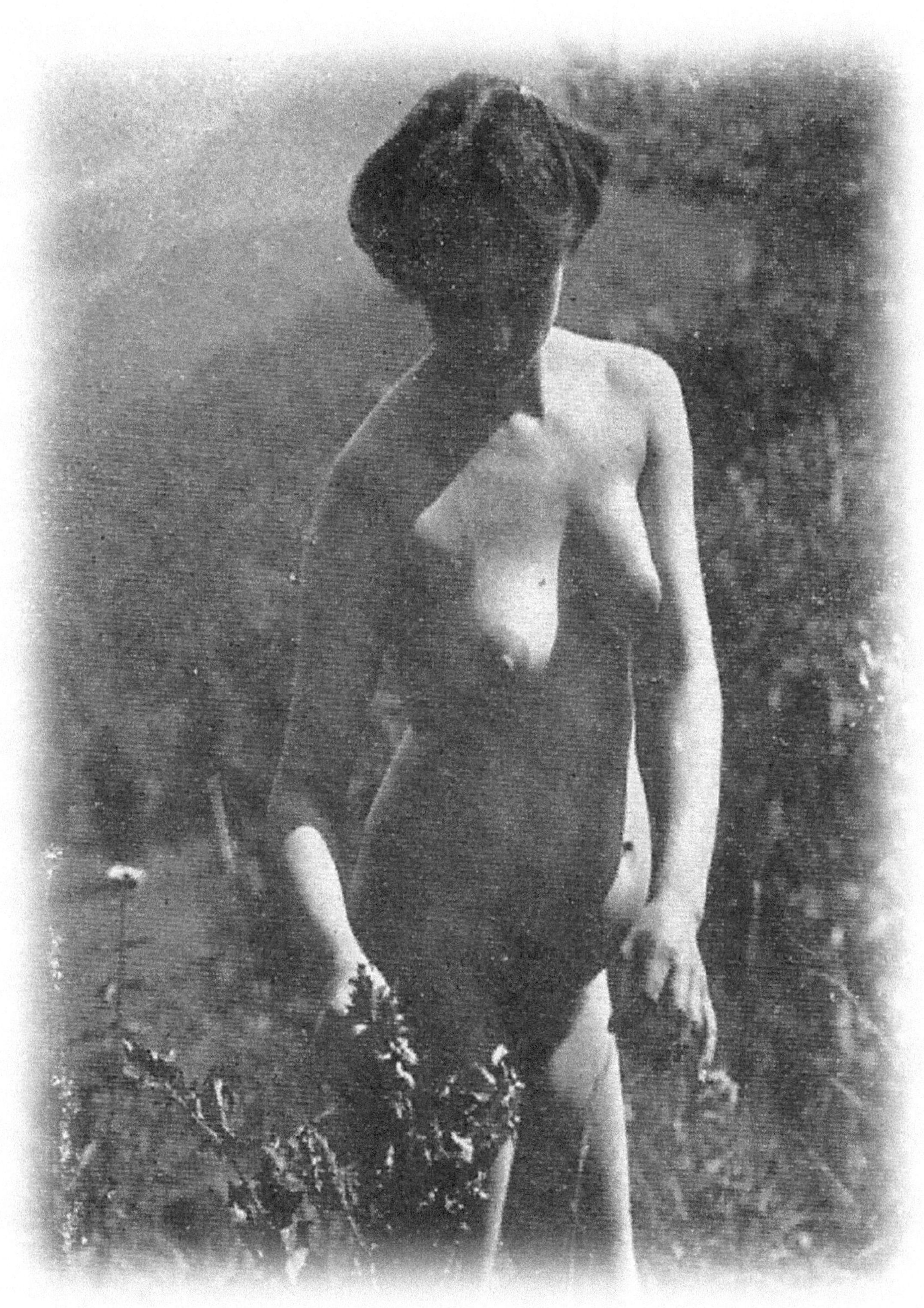

And in the fields and all…

And Willard looked at his wife and wondered how the years went wrong…

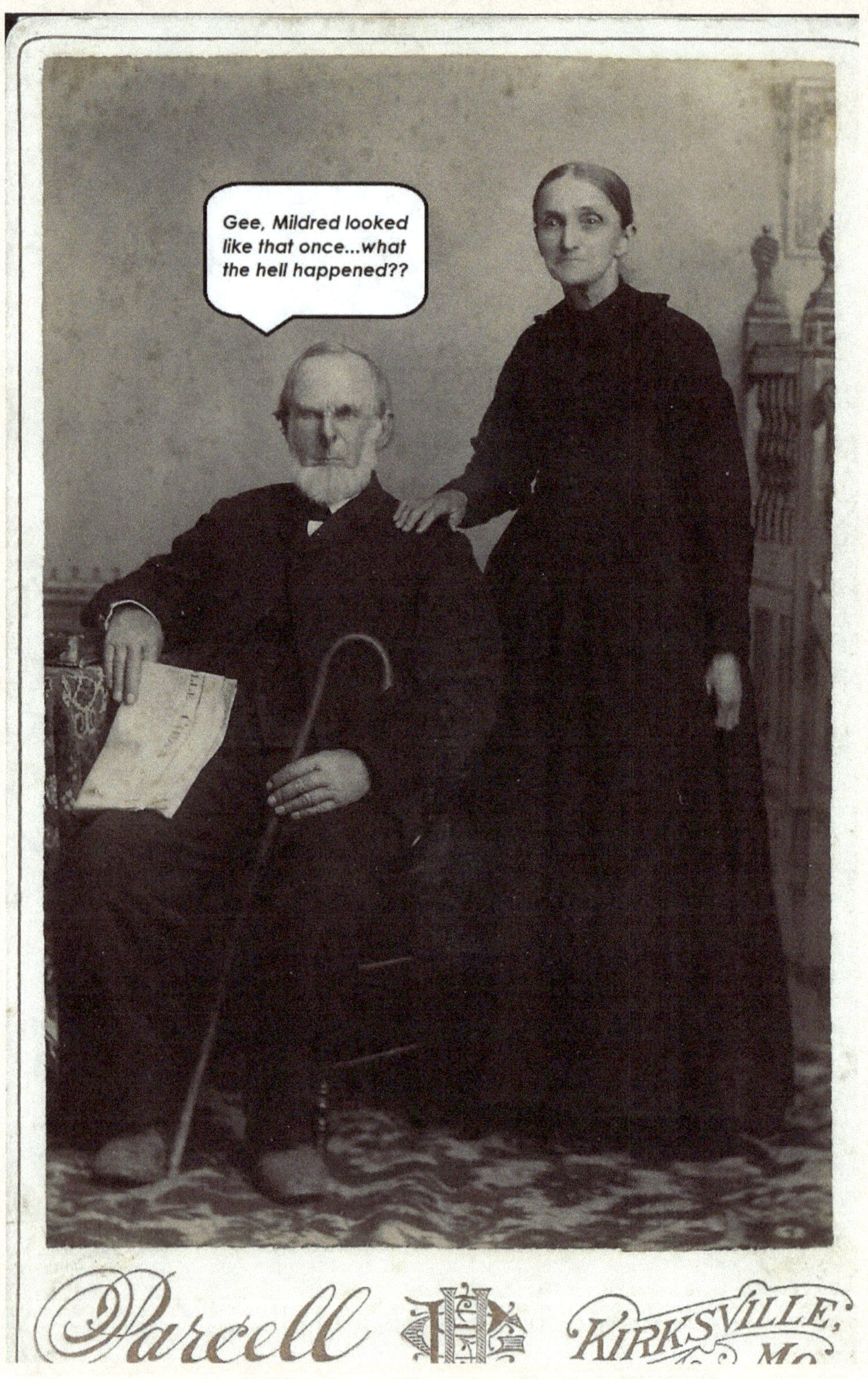

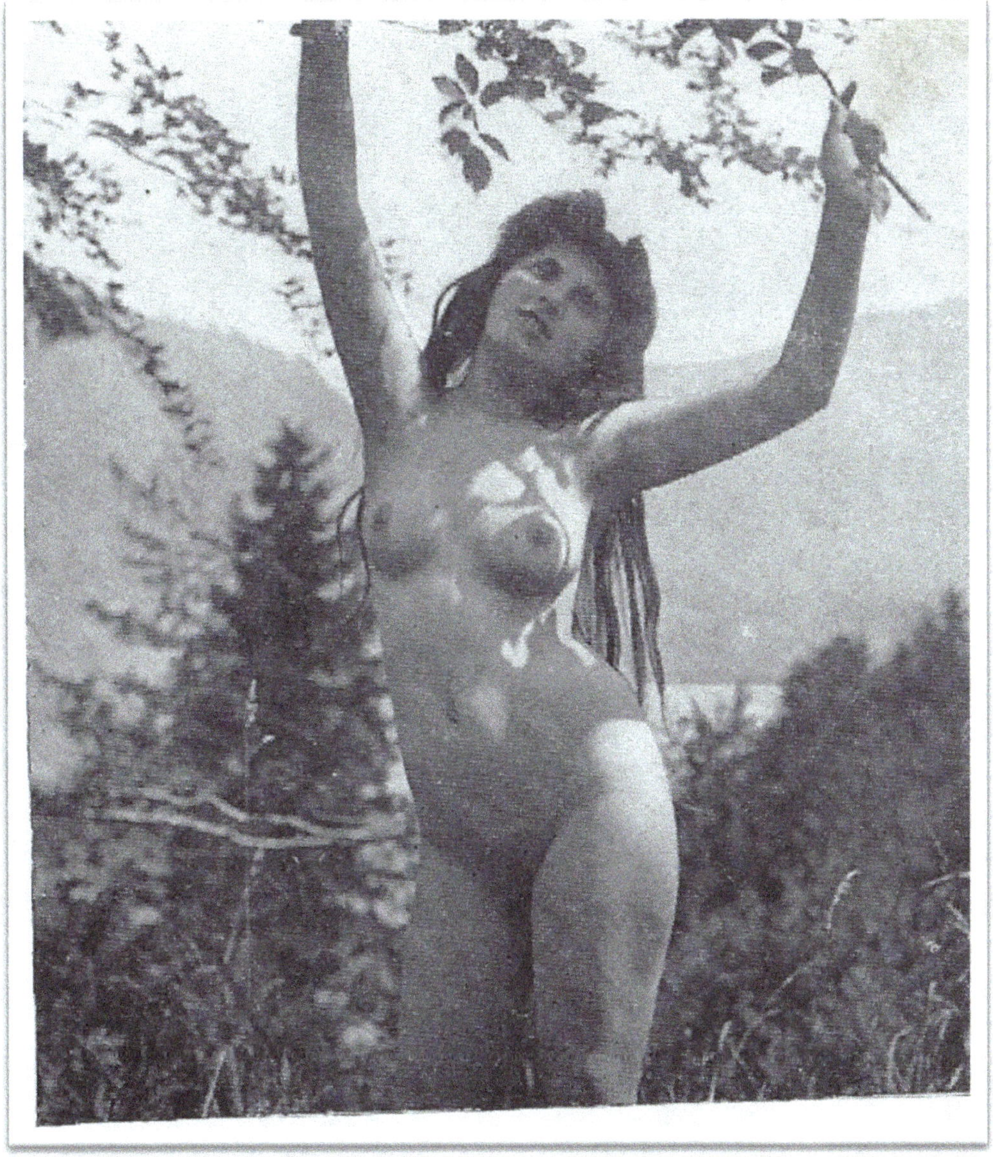

You just can't stop mother nature

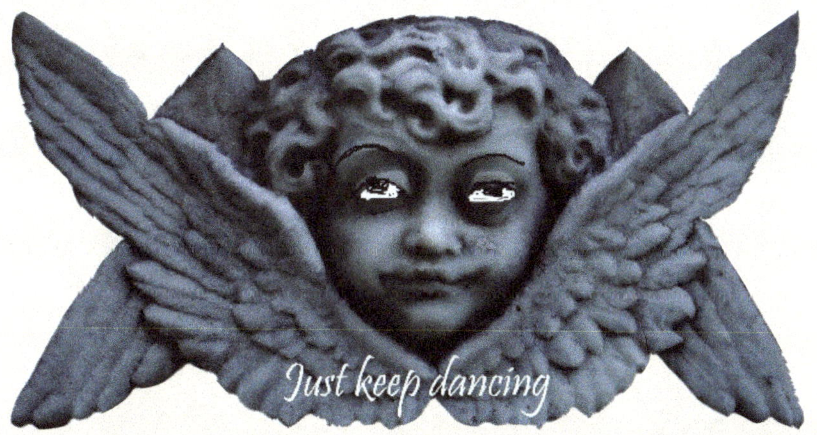

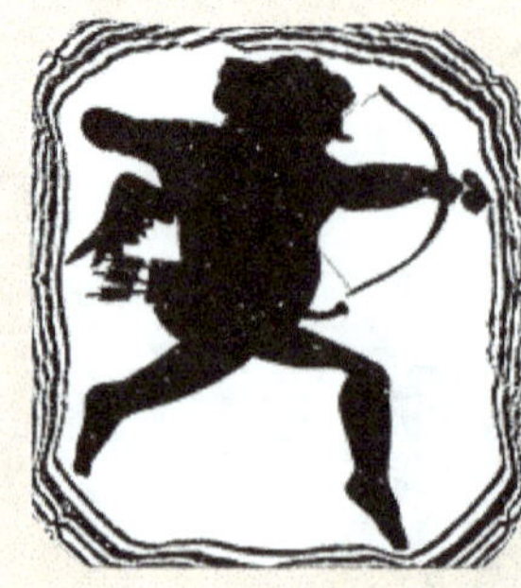

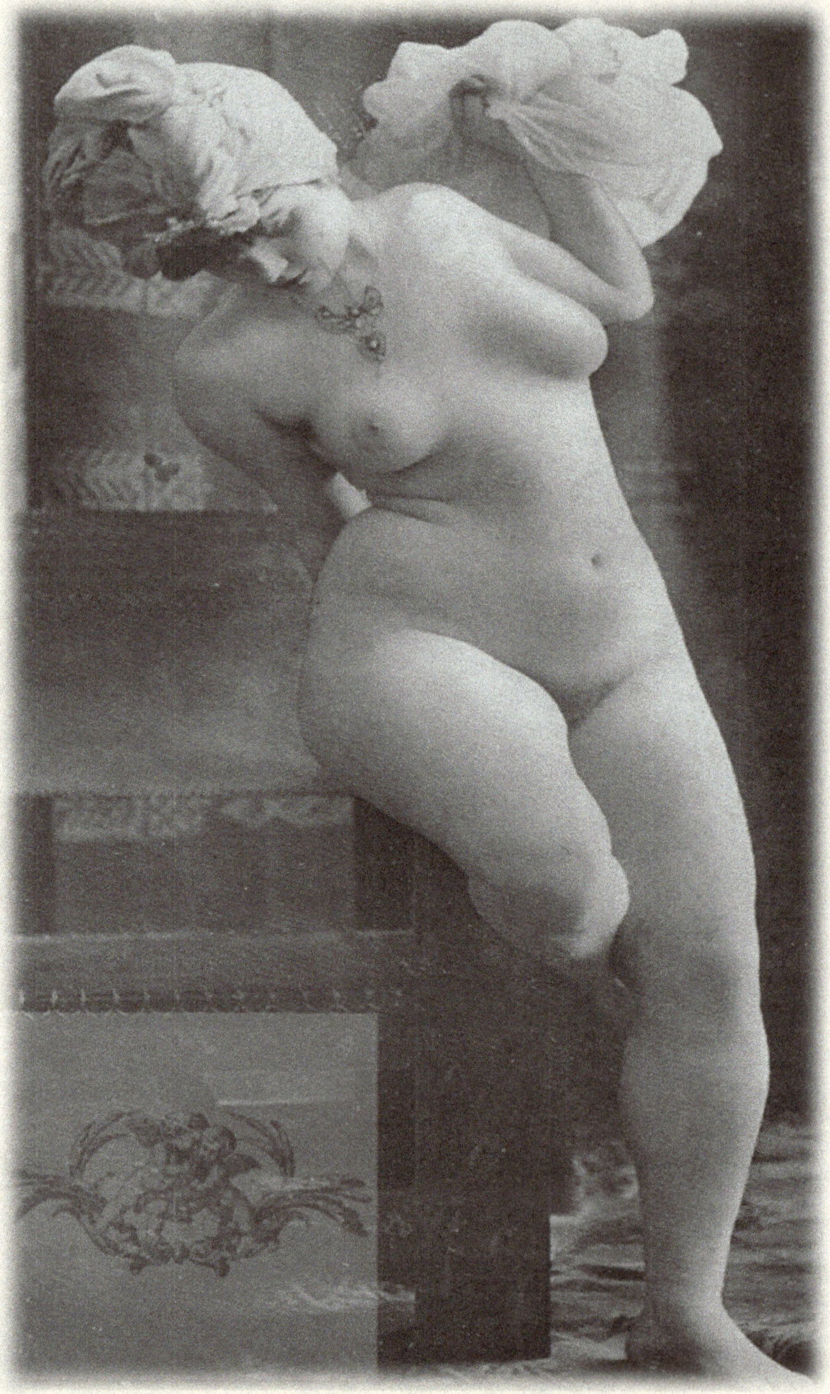

after the bath

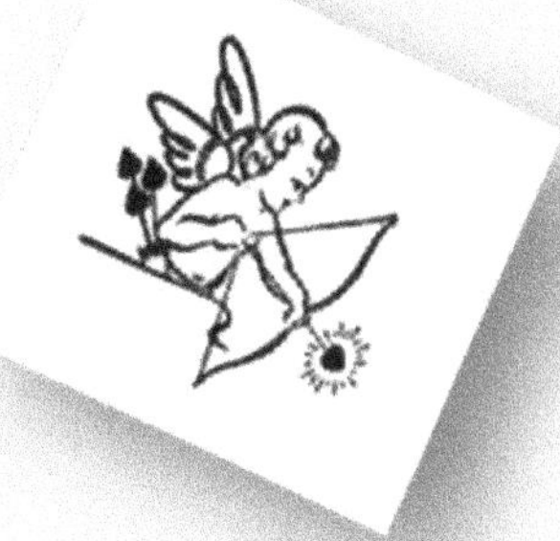

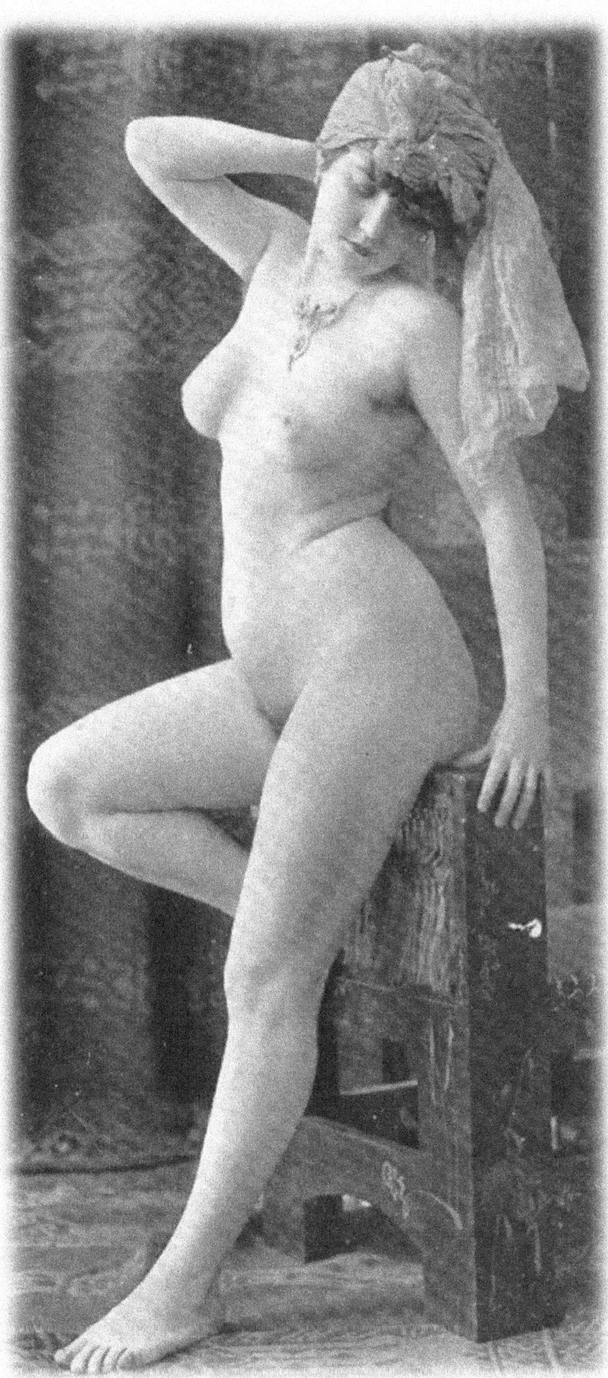

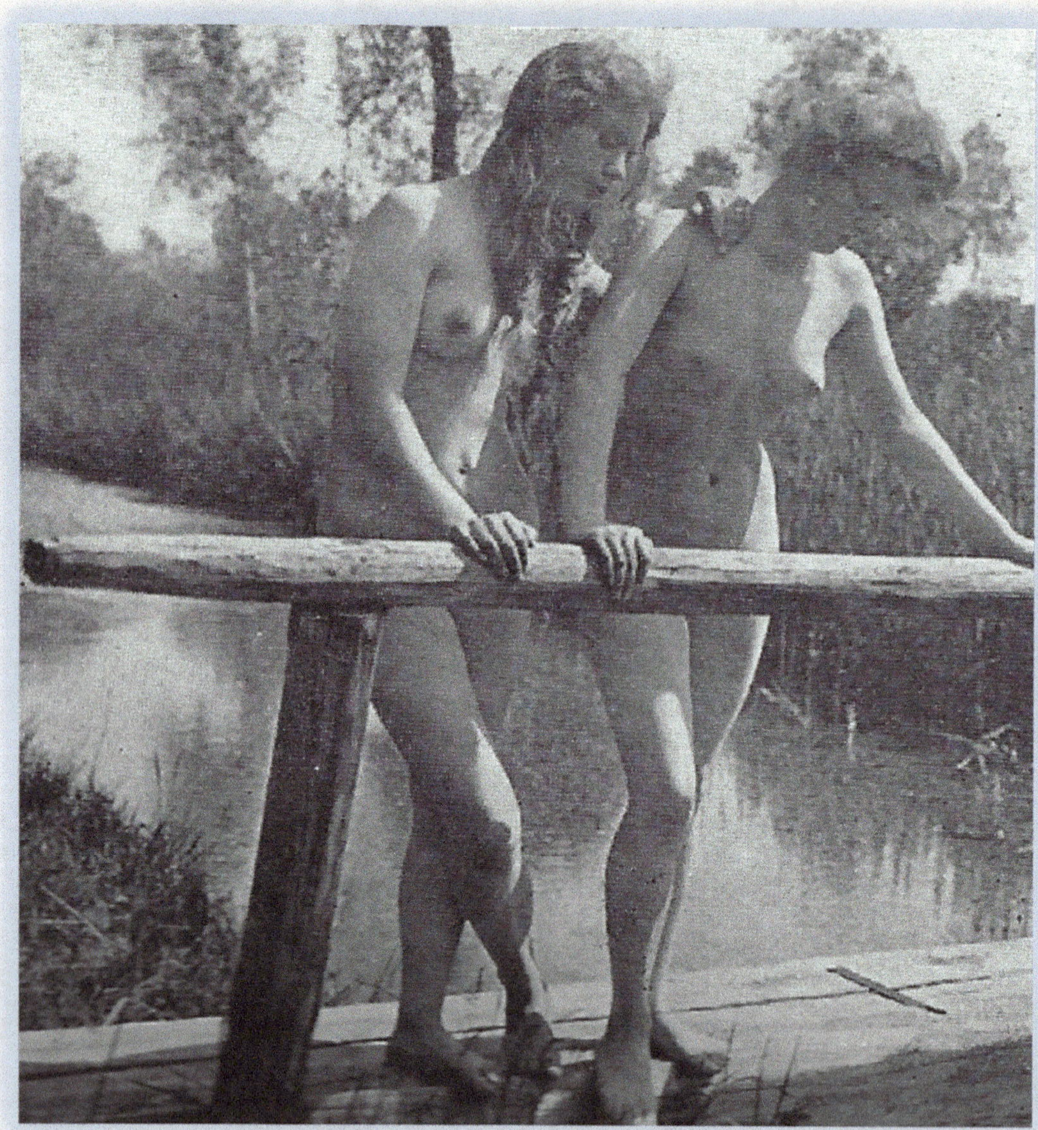

and on top of the bridge...

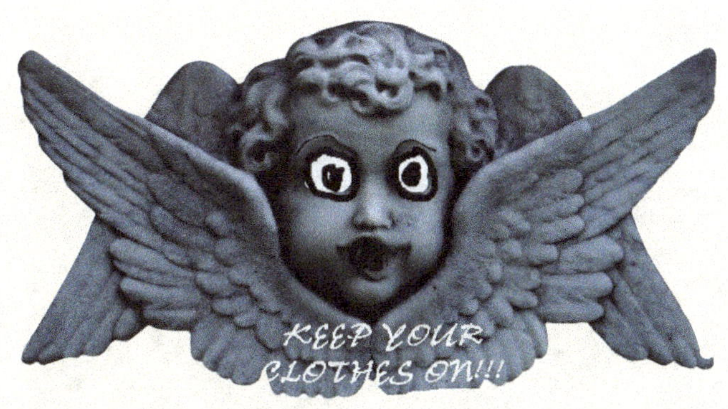
KEEP YOUR
CLOTHES ON!!!

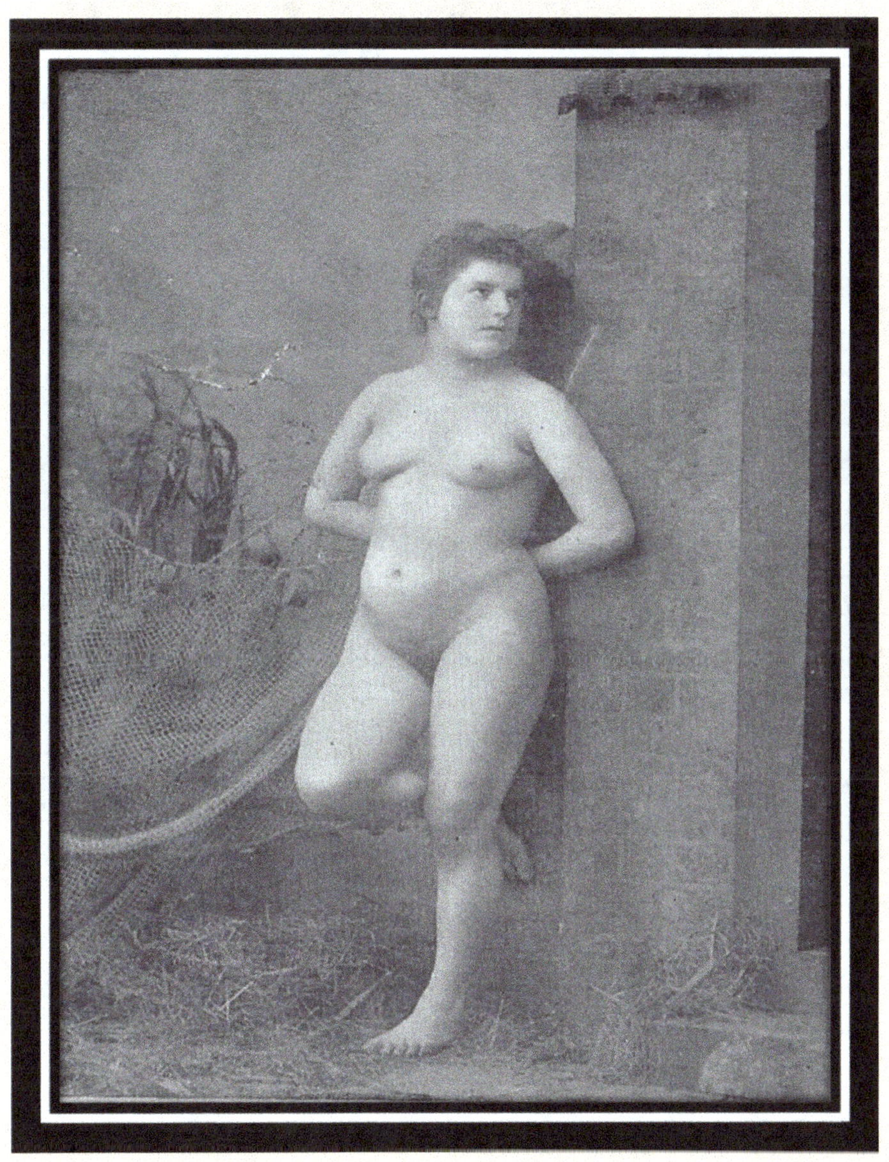

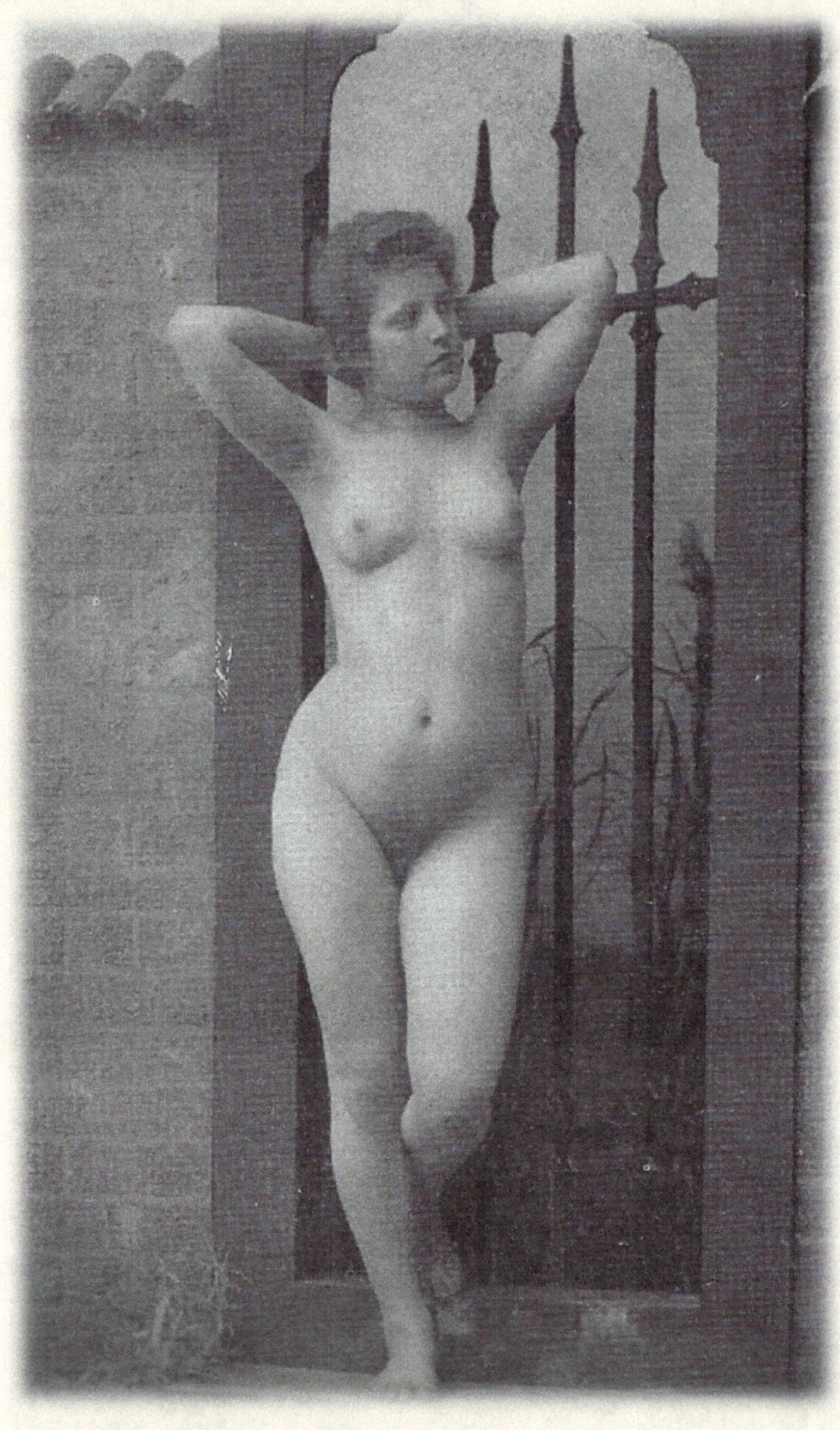

Gather ye rose-buds while ye may
Old Time is still a flying:

And this same flower that smiles today,
Tomorrow will be dying.

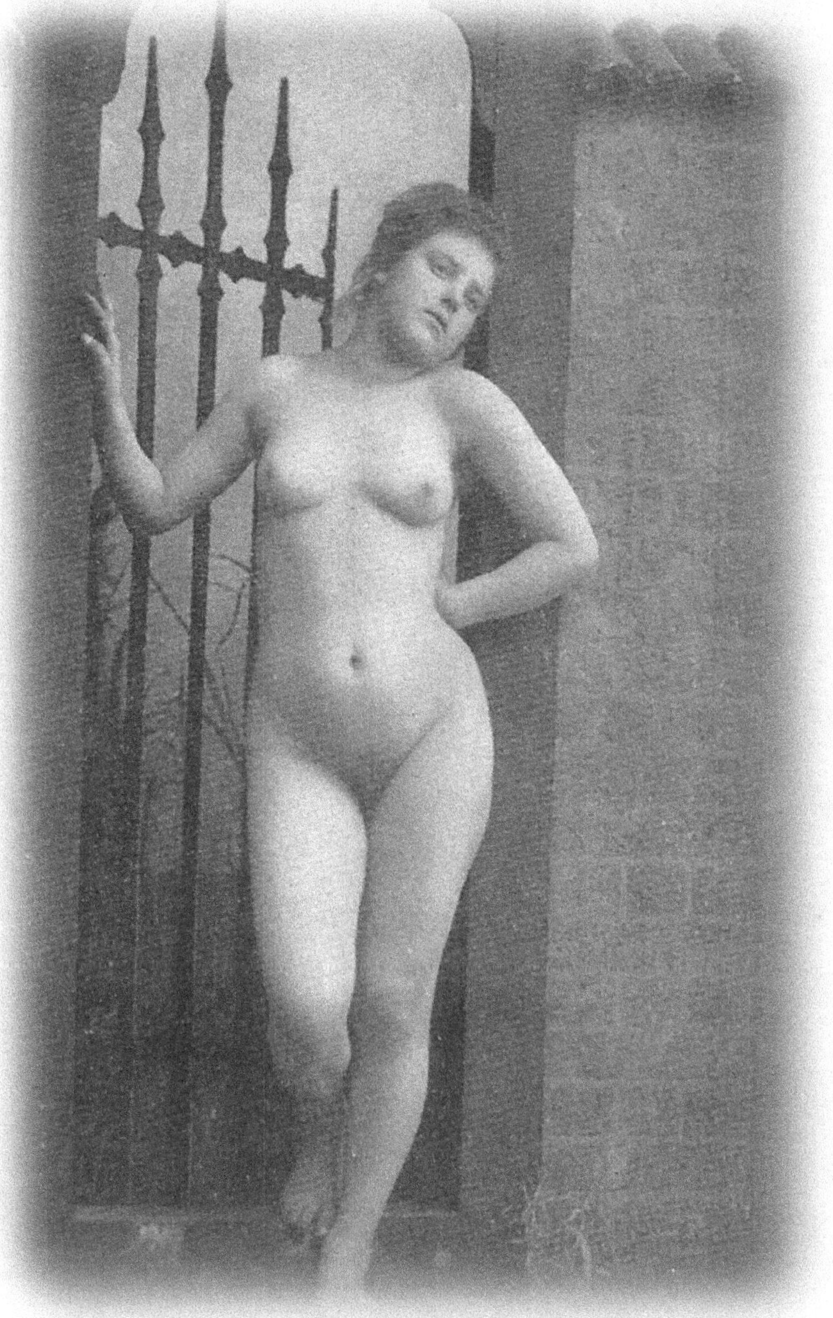

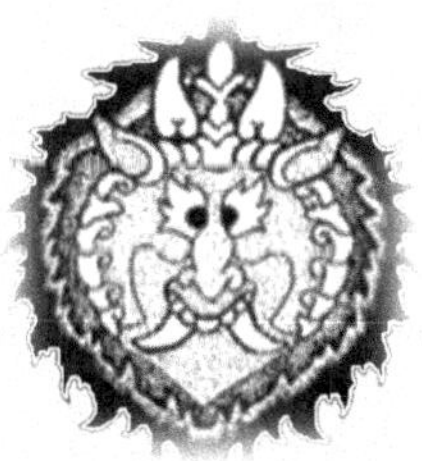

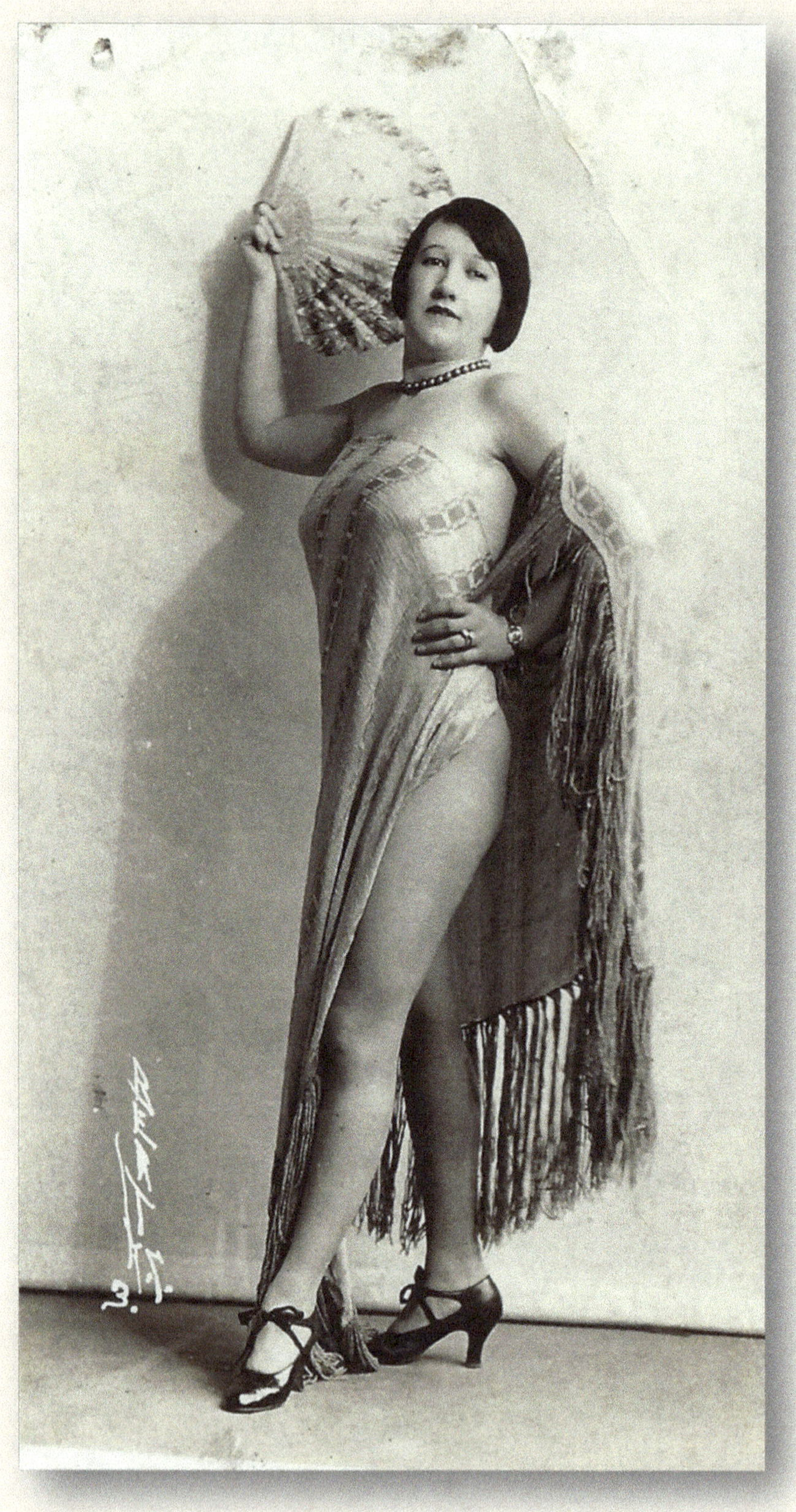

Not 1908, but 1920ish…

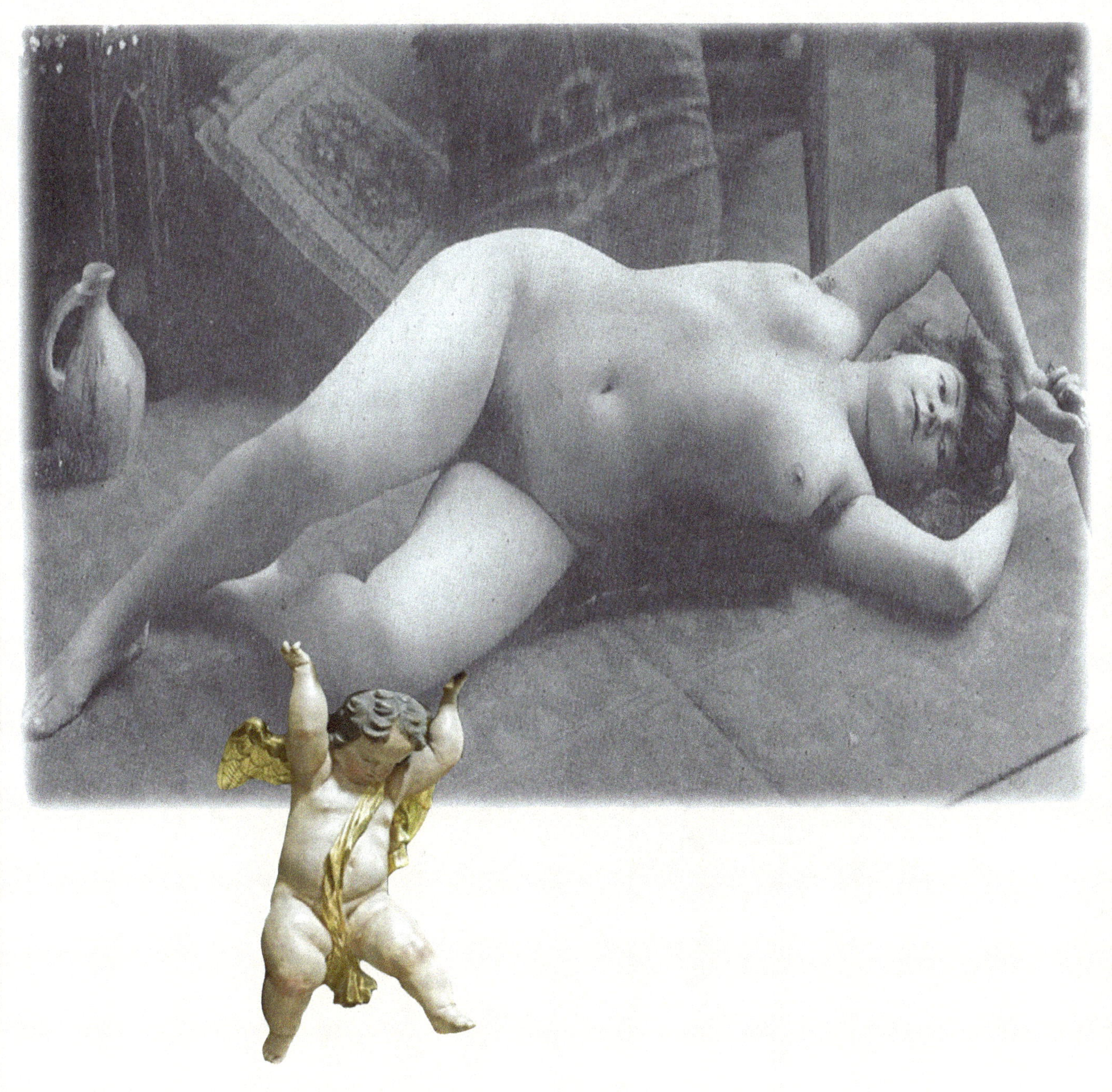

A small cherub holds the lady up…

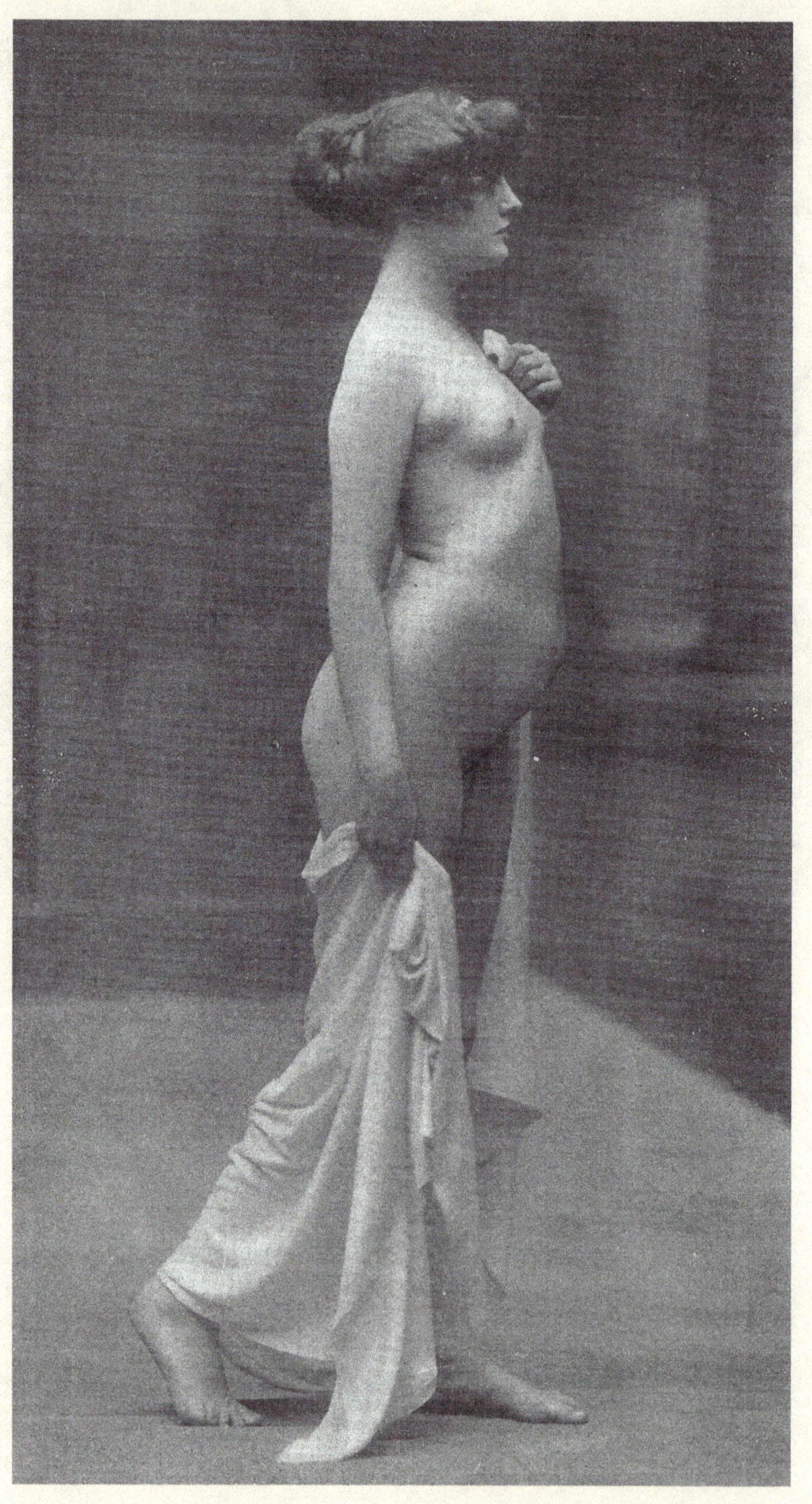

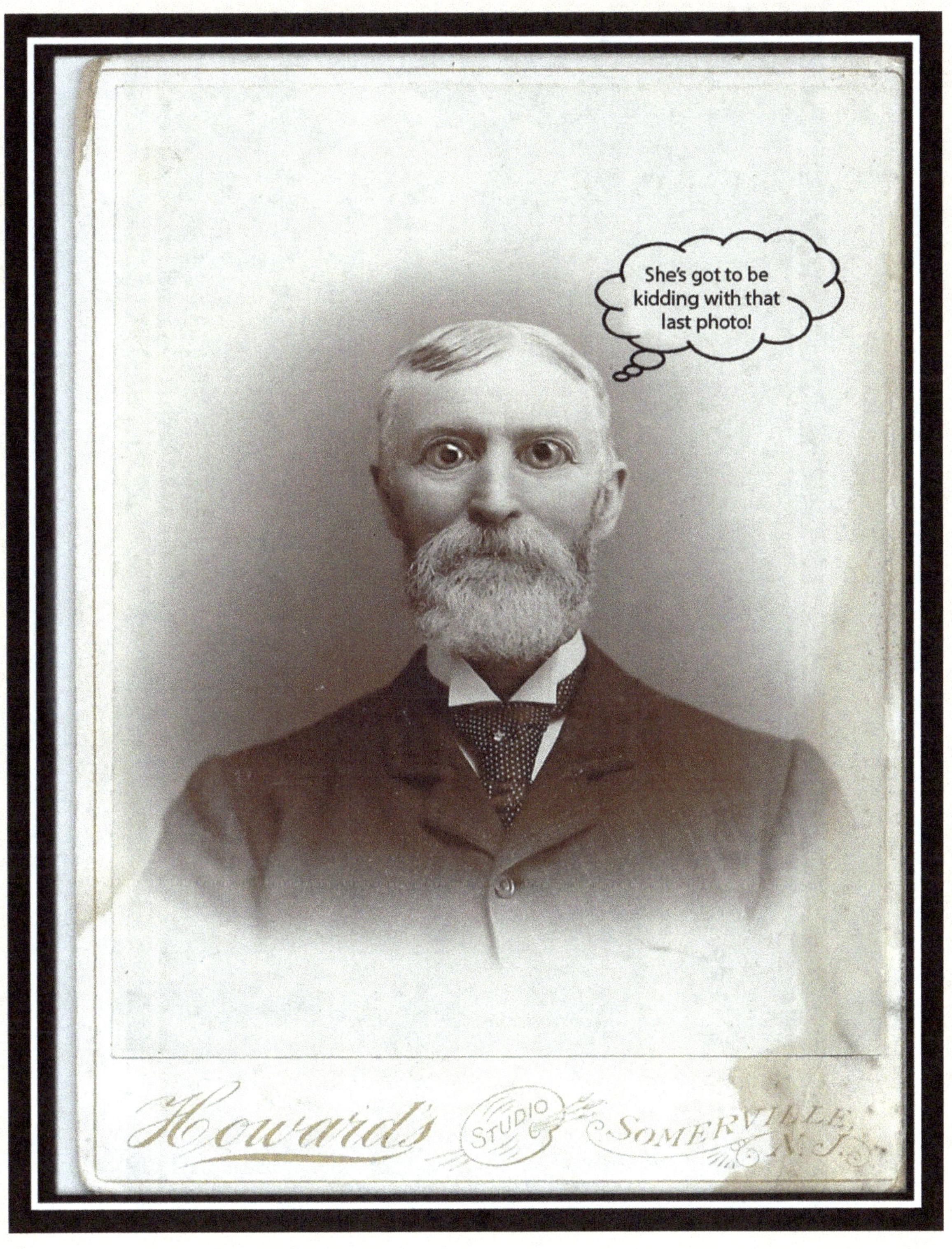

Mr. Chigpiddle did not approve of that last photo...
but who cares?

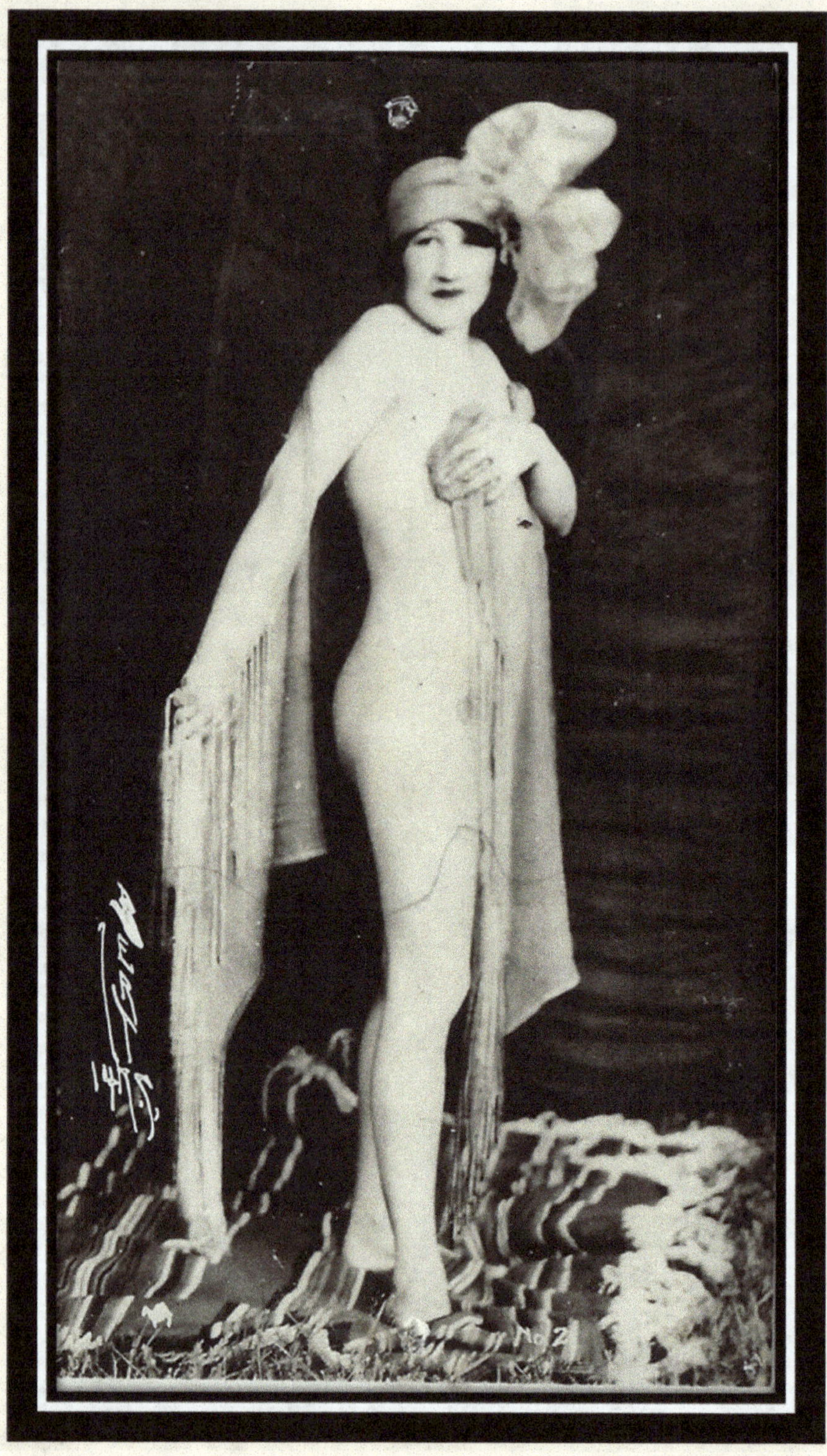

Love that bow!

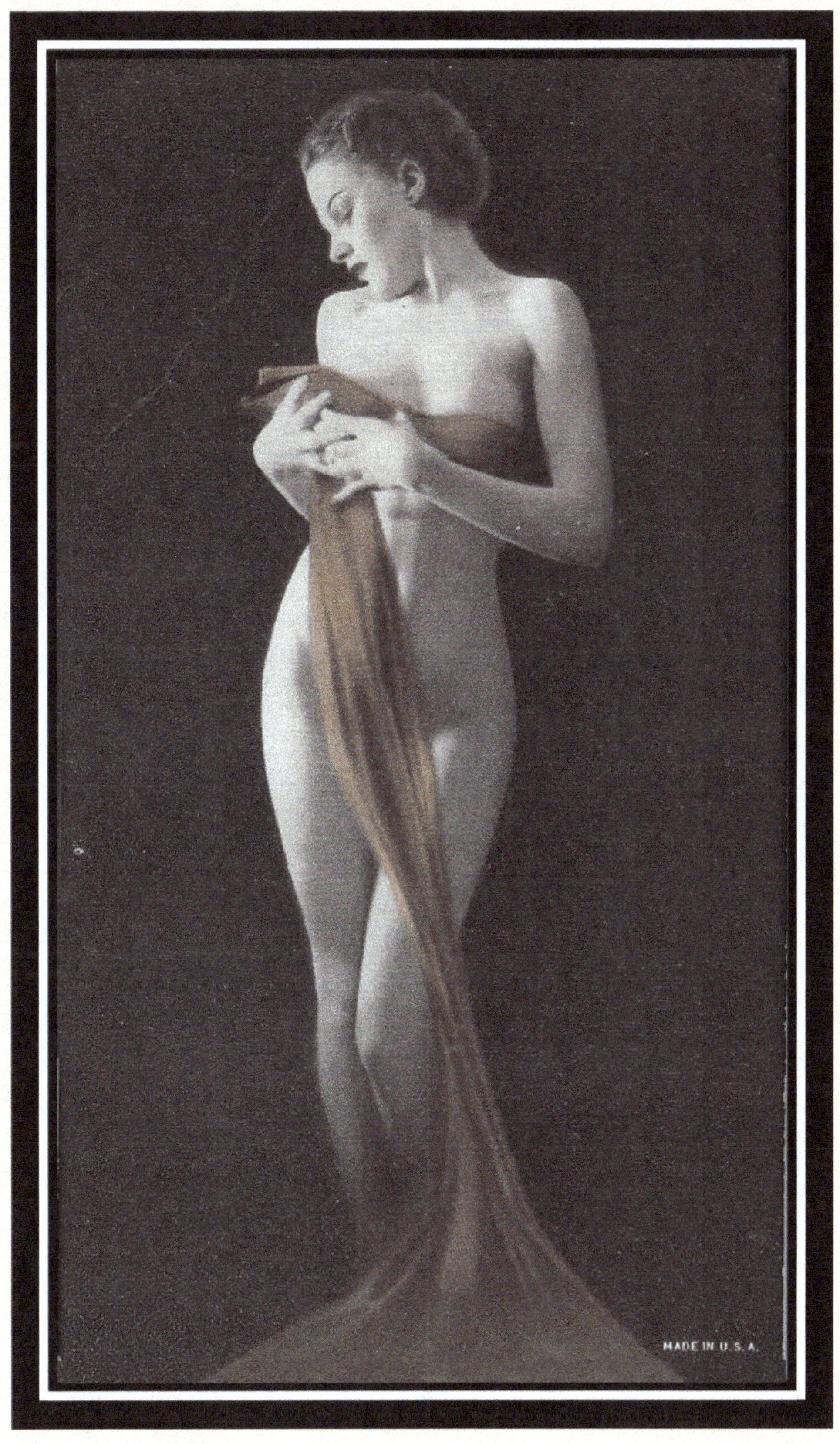

1930ish…

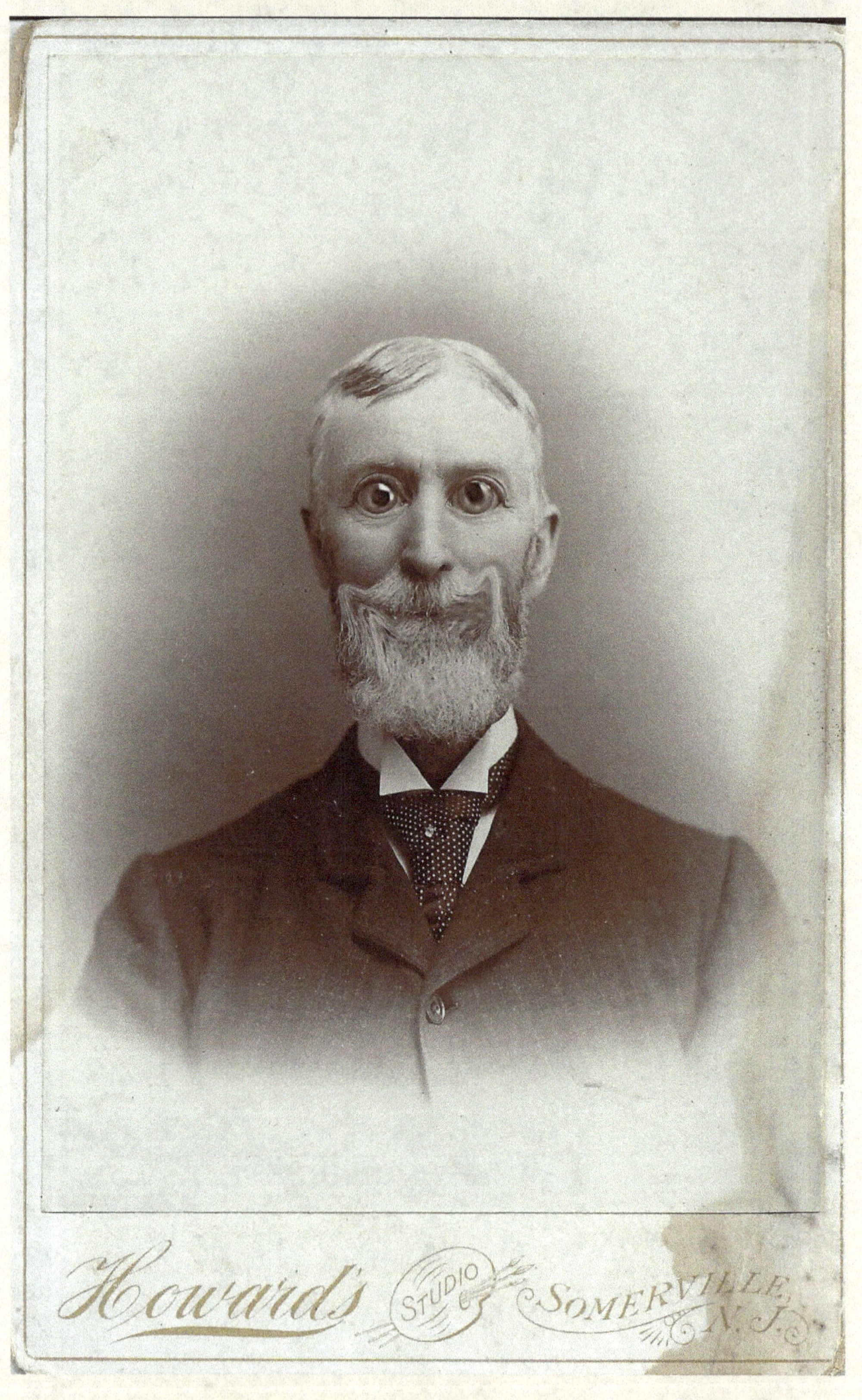

Mr. Chigpiddle like that last picture…you can tell by his smile.

And finally….

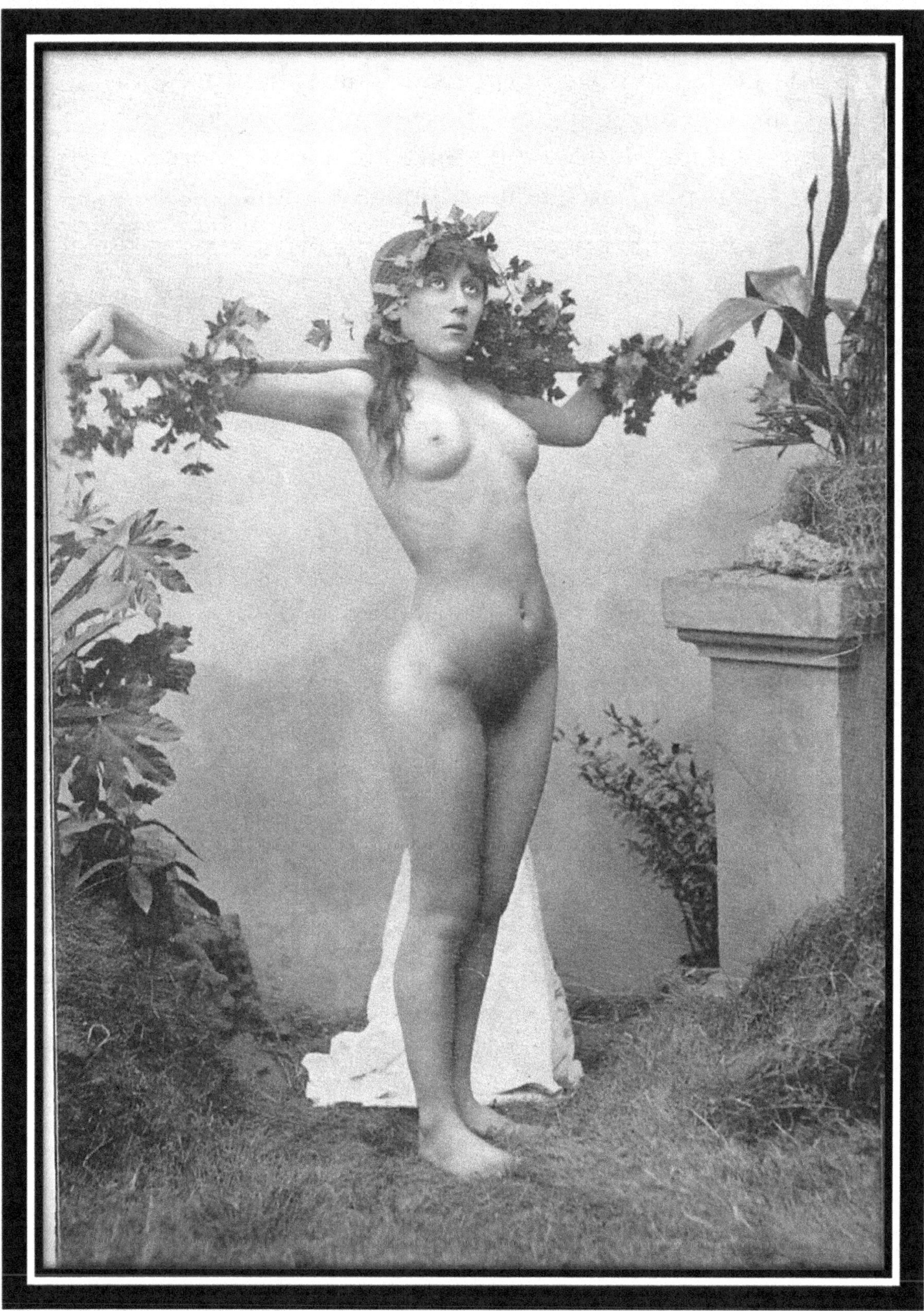

About the Author

Uma Bouschertz is an avid collector of antiques, old photographs, and porcelain. This is her first foray into creating a unique book from a collection of vintage nude photographs found in a lot of porcelain purchased at an antiques auction.

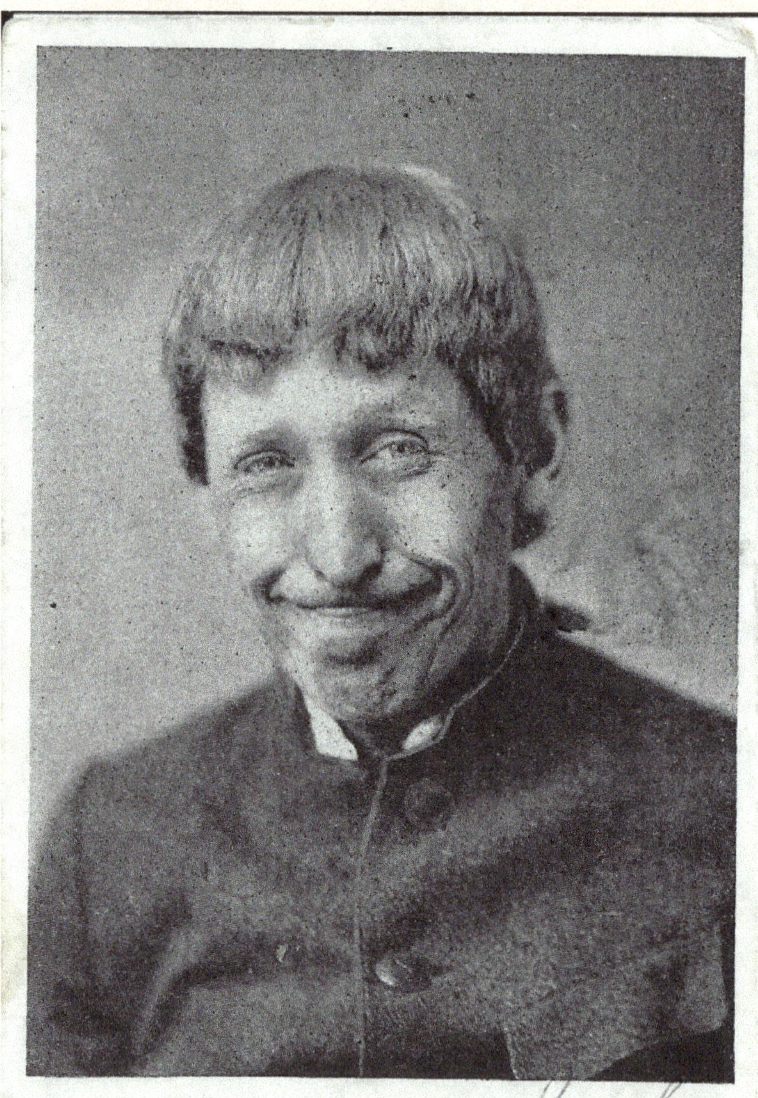

Don't Make Me Laugh; My Lips Are Chapped.

REALLY? Love, Uma

www.ingramcontent.com/pod-product-compliance
Lightning Source LLC
LaVergne TN
LVHW061257100826
845148LV00008B/1164
* 9 7 8 0 9 8 2 7 5 9 7 4 5 *